The Ishtar Ignition

Timothy Black

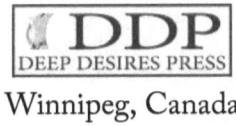

DDP

DEEP DESIRES PRESS

Winnipeg, Canada

Developmental editor: Craig Gibb
Proofreader: Francisco Feliciano

Published July 2023 by Deep Desires Press, an imprint of Story Perfect Inc.

Deep Desires Press
PO Box 51053 Tyndall Park
Winnipeg, Manitoba R2X 3B0
Canada

Visit http://www.deepdesirespress.com for more scorching hot erotica and erotic romance.

The Ishtar Ignition

Before

Charlotte Frost, captain of the airship *Harlot's Promise*, helped a sentient Doll named Tash flee from the clutches of the Matriarchy's soldiers. During the escape, they were both surprised when a separate personality took over and shifted the female Doll's body to a masculine form that went by Arslan, before reverting to the female configuration and personality. Following information buried deep in the automaton's mind, they flew across the Syrian Desert and revealed a hidden temple buried under the sands. They clutched each other tightly as the ship descended into the unknown darkness, their only haven from the pursuing forces.

Now

Chapter 1

The stars scattered across the canvas of the chilly night sky were blocked from sight as massive twin slabs of ceiling stone rumbled closed with a dread finality. The dry air felt lifeless and foreboding on the skin of the pair of figures who stood on the open deck of the airship as it continued down into the abyss.

Charlotte Frost, tantric mistress of the *Harlot's Promise*, guided her airship deeper into the dark depths of the ancient Temple of Ishtar that lay hidden beneath the ruins of the ancient city Arslan Tash. Through the control ruby on her tawny-brown forehead the aviatrix felt the wounds of the Liberty Ship as if they were her own. Fractures in the wood of the hull were like cuts on skin, and the libidium alloy skeleton that formed the superstructure and allowed flight hurt like bruised ribs after a prize fight. Despite the apparent lack of Matriarchy pursuers, Charlotte hadn't been able to risk the time to properly repair the ship after jettisoning the seaward sail in the frantic escape from the floating city of Godmother. Although the starward sail and the engine pontoons were still able to direct the elegant ship the extra stresses from compensating for its hobbled maneuverability since then had piled the smaller injuries together to form into larger problems. Charlotte was careful to descend at minimum speed, to not aggravate the ship's injuries any further.

But as complete darkness enveloped the world, the aviatrix feared she might have all the time in the world now to repair the *Harlot's Promise*, trapped under a forgotten patch of the Syrian Desert.

Charlotte hugged the six-foot tall alabaster and gold Doll in her arms closer, the automaton's artificial skin soft and warm from the magic that animated her. Unlike the mindless machines commonly used by tantric aviatrixes to supply their erotic engineering needs, this Doll was no mere sex toy. She was a self-aware construct, an artificial intelligence capable of love and hate, resistance and consent. Charlotte had initially been taken aback at the discovery of true life existing within the construct, but it was hard for the captain to imagine her companion otherwise now. The mixture of a guileless and tawdry mind woven with a fierce and almost instantaneous loyalty to Charlotte had ignited far more passion in the captain for the Doll than her physical form alone could have done. There was a rebellious streak through it all that was all the more alluring to the captain after the Matriarchal conformity her ex-wife had staidly clung to. Tash was more than just beautiful; she was exciting in a way that promised there would be no pain at the end of the road.

The sentient machine wore a ruffled off the shoulder white dress with yellow flowers, complete with goldenrod bonnet on her bald head as well as matching lace gloves and shoes, an outfit she had picked out with equal parts taste and innocence. Tash had fled to the captain wearing substantially less, and if she transformed into her male form, Arslan, it would rip the dress to shreds with the mass redistribution. But the Arslan fragment seemed content to slumber in the background, allowing Tash full control of the body for now.

Although apparently named after the ruins above, the female-form Tash and her male alter ego, Arslan, had been unable to provide any information on the dangers lurking within the temple. The composite souls that inhabited the Doll were able to give them entry to the hidden depths, but that appeared to be the extent of their powers over the place. They seemed to be as ignorant as Charlotte about how and why they existed, and their connection with the forgotten ruins.

The captain shuddered as the darkness pressed in during the slow descent. Yet in her arms she discovered she held an unexpected treasure. Tash's skin was emitting a dim, pearlescent glow from just under the surface, flickering like an angel in the abyss. It wasn't much, but the faint light helped fight back the claustrophobia that threatened to grip Charlotte and made the aviatrix feel like the moon had graced her with an embrace. The Doll felt her captain tense, and turned her head back, concern marring her mechanically perfect features.

"Mistress?" Tash asked, her tone probing. "What is wrong?"

Nearly invisible lines of silver runes shone under the

Doll's skin, and below that a complicated interior of pistons and gears of worked golden alloy gave her the appearance of life, the clockwork visible through the malleable translucent skin covering her joints. But without the magic animating and softening the ivory muscle plates that comprised her frame she would have been just another machine, albeit a spectacularly complicated one. Normal Dolls of steel and brass were obedient sex objects used as one would any other tool. But whoever had designed Tash had created a true work of art, using a construction material rarer than any jewel: a human soul.

Or rather, multiple souls.

"You're radiant, Tash!" Charlotte marveled, pushing her companion slightly away so she could marvel at how the Doll lit her dress from within. Tash was taller than her captain by a good four or five inches, and with the automaton's larger breasts and shoulders Charlotte could have easily been intimidated. But the Doll had shown nothing but loyalty and gentleness after their escape, so it was easy for Charlotte to forget how much smaller she was than her companion.

"I am flattered, mistress, but I am not sure how your admiration pertains to our situation," the Doll shrugged, her bare shoulders and collarbone depression a lovely arch and delicate depth that tempted toward the other, more sinful bits.

Charlotte stared into the featureless golden orbs that served as Tash's eyes, set in her perfect face. The captain laughed at herself.

"I forget you're not flesh and blood, thus not

constrained as much as we mere mortals," Charlotte said, stroking the Doll's cheek with a finger. It was as pliant as real skin, and the clockwork ticking along inside felt like a pulse. "We're in the dark. Quite literally. And your skin is emitting a low degree of luminescence; not enough to see more than a few feet, but still extraordinary. You look…heavenly."

"My appetites are full of sin though," Tash said, smiling mischievously with her golden lips that slowly melted into a frown. "But before our feast takes us, you require true light. Otherwise, your fear will grow, defeating my most lascivious and tempting seductions."

"Fair point," Charlotte allowed, breaking their embrace. "Fortunately, this isn't the first time I've found myself lost in a moonless night."

Charlotte sent a thought through the *Harlot's Promise* to power down the pontoon engines and pushed power into the libidium frame to halt their descent. As they came to a stable hover, the captain searched through her cabin for the equipment she was after. The quartz ship lights spaced around the Liberty Ship were dimmer than they should have been, as if the darkness was a malevolent creature consuming the crystalline luminescence. But even in the strange gloom Charlotte was able to locate the polished mahogany box she was looking for.

"Have you ever met a fairy before?" she asked Tash with an impish grin as she emerged from her cabin back onto the deck.

"Are those not merely of myth and legend?" Tash replied, her gaze lingering on the box suspiciously.

"Not anymore."

Charlotte opened the box. Inside rested twenty or thirty agate marbles of different colors, varying between a half and full inch in diameter, packed in tight with each other. Tash could detect the whisper of libidium running through the variegation of the small orbs, glittering to her senses like diamonds to the eyes. Someone had gone to considerable trouble to polish all the stones to a glass-like sheen; together, the mahogany box and shiny treasure within would have been the pride of any princeling. Charlotte grinned at Tash's confused look and leaned close to the mystic marbles, whispering an incantation laced with power.

For a moment nothing happened. Then, as if a flock of birds waking to the dawn, the stones shuddered, jostling together as they reacted to the aviatrix's magic. Sparks sputtered at the center of each, growing to a steady glow that created a kaleidoscopic light that grew stronger as the marbles bumped against each other. Another whispered word sent them floating gently out of the box, a rainbow of miniscule lights, each shimmering a different color. They orbited the aviatrix and her clockwork courtesan in a glowing cloud, tethered to their creator by lines of invisible magic so delicate even Tash could barely detect them.

"Mistress," Tash breathed in wonderment. "You never cease to amaze."

The aviatrix smiled wide. "Despite the promises in my storybooks when I was a little girl, I never did find any fairy kingdoms. But I'm too stubborn to allow reality to spoil my fun."

The cloud of fae lights widened their circle at Charlotte's whispered command, casting their multi-colored illumination over the expansive chamber.

Above, the giant stone slabs that had allowed entry to the cavern hidden beneath the temple ruins were locked back in place; the relatively crude powered slides that had moved them looked as they'd withstood centuries, if not millennia of existence. The lights revealed the space below to be a cavern originally, with stalactites hanging from the unmodified portions of the roof, relics of a bygone age where the desert had been a lush forest.

In width the rectangular cavern was about forty or fifty yards from the ship's hull in each direction, the boundaries set by dusty sandstone brick walls seemingly as ancient as the device above. The glow of the fae lights was unable to penetrate the gloom of the far corners of the cavern, but as she looked around it was apparent to her that Charlotte had stumbled onto a massive secret, in all meanings of the word. During their approach the aviatrix had detected aetheric energy permeating the ruins, more than she'd ever seen before. To even try and don the special goggles that allowed her to see the mystic currents would likely blind her, such was the intensity level. The Matriarchy had never operated much in this part of the world, and she'd not heard of any sister-captains soaring this way. Charlotte had always assumed it was some sort of unconscious choice or bias; despite their dizzying array of ethnicities, the Matriarchy had concentrated its efforts since inception two decades ago on bringing about societal change and female liberation in Europe. Although many assumed it was just because they were farther along the industrial development road and therefore more of a threat to those who dwelt in the skies, the obvious and easily detected energy of the ruins revealed that as a convenient lie. The Crone Council had kept them well clear of the Middle East intentionally. If these temple ruins were so rife with mystic energy, what other wonders might be held in the cradle of humanity?

The fae lights zoomed below the *Harlot's Promise*, revealing the packed dirt of the ground and confirming Charlotte's suspicions.

The wreckage of a massive Matriarchy airship littered the ground below.

The design was unmistakably one of Charlotte's sisterhood, although she'd never seen one so large or utilitarian before. The fleet of Liberty Ships the Matriarchy generally favored were sleeker and smaller, prioritizing speed and beauty in equal parts over size. Grounders were an ever-present threat, and the various governments of man had been hard at work developing weapons that could down any craft lacking sufficient maneuverability.

But the wreck below was at least four times as large as the *Harlot's Promise*, with the brutal simplicity of an untrained craftswoman's hand. The impact with the ground had splint it asunder like an overripe melon, revealing all its flaws. Like the jagged teeth of a nightmare, the broken hull jutted up in various places; the crystalline engine had obviously detonated in the crash, throwing debris across the otherwise featureless ground below. Although it covered the floor directly beneath, there were clear spaces beyond its impact site that remained free of detritus. The tangle of brass and iron was rusted despite the desert clime, and the broken wooden hull and deck pieces were fragile with apparent desiccation, indicating a few decades since disaster befell the forgotten craft. Holding her breath as if submerging beneath the ocean, the captain ordered the ship to come in for a landing.

Angling the *Harlot's Promise* as close as she dared to the wreckage, Charlotte strained to pick out details in the half-light to no avail. The frustrated aviatrix was tempted to don the goggles, if only for a short look. But there was too much danger that the resultant feedback would burn out her mystic senses as surely as staring into the sun would destroy her eyes. At least the captain's link to the ship through the control ruby allowed enough awareness that she was able to bring them down relatively gently on the landing struts that extended out with a hiss of their hydraulics. Or, rather, that was what she expected. In the last twenty feet before landing there was a sudden power loss in the flight aura. Although Charlotte was able to push more power through the system to compensate, they still came in harder than she expected. Both she and her companion stumbled as the ship landed in like a ton of bricks.

The *Harlot's Promise* groaned in complaint at the rough landing, but it held together despite the protestations. Charlotte untangled her higher mental functions from the Liberty Ship, her mind refocusing as if from a dream.

"Mistress? I feel...so very odd..." Tash murmured.

"It's all right Tash, I just didn't expect—"

Turning toward her friend, Charlotte gave a startled scream as she caught sight of the Doll's face.

The sculpted beauty of Tash was melting and intermixing like a set of candles thrown into a fire. Her form was in a state of sudden flux; Charlotte lunged forward to steady her swaying companion only for her fingers to sink into the ivory plating that comprised Tash's muscles. The magic that animated the Doll was pulsing in an uncontrolled surge. The captain watched in helpless horror as Tash's face melted to her male form, Arslan, before shifting to other faces, older females, and then back to Tash.

"Lilith's tit!" Charlotte swore in awestruck terror.

She'd recognized the other faces that Tash had manifested.

"Tash! Arslan! Whichever of you that can hear me!" Charlotte shouted, trying to focus the Doll's attention on her with snapping fingers. "Hold on! Pull yourself together, damn it! I need you!"

The automaton's ivory flesh solidified for a moment, and Tash's face boiled to the top of the surging mass of her head, silently screaming in panic.

"You stay with me, you hear?" Charlotte demanded. Bereft of anything else she could think of, the aviatrix did the only thing that came to mind.

She kissed Tash.

The moment her dark umber lips touched the Doll's golden ones the automaton lunged forward, hungry with need. Tash's face began to stabilize; her mistress's lips were an anchor to the real world, and her form slowly settled down through a series of ripples like a pebble dropped into water. Despite the weight of the automaton, the captain cradled Tash as she laid her companion down on the deck, still kissing her passionately. The Doll's skin calmed, becoming firm to the touch again. Finally, Charlotte broke the embrace, reeling from the sexual venom in Tash's saliva, her nether regions suddenly craving her new lover's fingers and tongue. The clockwork courtesan's lustful venom had been meant to enthrall the world's leaders, but the effect was equally seductive on any other person, even a tantric engineer.

Tash stared back up, the adoration for her mistress warring with a confused dread.

"What just happened to me?" the Doll asked, her voice as small and vulnerable as a child's.

Charlotte shook her head with a frown, drawing Tash in protectively. The automaton's skin was solid and warm again. "Honestly? No clue. What's the last thing you remember?"

"The release of your fairy lights, but after that…is as if an echo of a dream," the Doll said, her voice muffled as she turned her head and burrowed into Charlotte's breasts. Although she didn't have the cleavage of the Doll there was still enough there for a comfortable hiding place.

"Hey, careful there," Charlotte chided. "You've got a pointy chin, you know."

A muffled giggle and Tash looked back up at her mistress. Her face was beatific in the way that priests envisioned the divine, but it was contorted with dread.

"I am very frightened," she said.

The simple statement did more to chill the captain's blood than the wreckage surrounding them or being trapped in a lonely cavern under the desert. Charlotte hadn't counted on the Doll having all the answers, but up to this point the automaton had seemed so certain, so strangely knowledgeable when asked directly about this place. Lacking a memory from before she activated back on Godmother, Tash had acted more out of self-preservation than any inherent programming when she'd fled the flying city. In the gentler slivers of time between danger, the Doll had shown more interest in getting closer to Charlotte than of exploring her past. The mystery of what had come before was of little interest compared to the feelings burgeoning between the pair of rebels.

The aviatrix leaned down and kissed Tash gently on her forehead.

"We'll face the monsters together," Charlotte promised with a reassuring smile. But there was a pit of worry in her stomach.

"As you say, mistress," Tash said, reaching her delicate hand up to stroke away one of Charlotte's dark curls from her face. The trust, the utter and complete belief in her captain, scared the hell out of Charlotte. There was a strange thrill being with someone who was so loyal, so certain that you knew the answers. It was intoxicating and terrifying at the same time. It made her want to be a better woman, to crusade against any and all that would cause sorrow to Tash.

The aviatrix helped her pale consort up, dusting off the automaton's ruffled dress. The scarlet flight leathers that Charlotte wore were much sturdier in comparison, barely showing any scuff marks.

"Speaking of monsters…what manner of misfortune do

you suppose is responsible for that airship's demise?" Tash asked, nodding toward the massive wreck. The fae lights drifted over the shattered hull, picking out the carefully painted name of the doomed Matriarchy vessel: *Lilith's Embrace.*

"You don't know?" Charlotte asked. "Tash, you literally made the earth move to get us in here."

Tash gave a very human sigh of frustration.

"When you request that I complete a task, I will do my utmost to accomplish it. But I have no recollection of *how* I do it. Evidently my subconscious protocols obey your whims more readily than mine. I know not how I raise my arm, simply that it is willed and thus it happens; the same applies to opening the ruins for entry."

"Wait…if I give a command…you believe it can get past whatever is blocking your memories?" Charlotte asked with growing excitement.

"That appears to be the truth of it. But pray tell, what precisely did you have in mind, mistress?" Tash asked coquettishly.

"Ah, if only," Charlotte said, clearing her throat. "Later. For now, 'needs must when the devil drives,' as they say. Tell me this, Tash: what happened here?"

They both stared at each other for a moment. Charlotte held her breath, hoping for some remnant of a forgotten memory to surface in the Doll, escaping the intractable internal glacier that held all of Tash's knowledge.

There was nothing.

"This feels…awkward," Tash said after a moment of

them staring at each other with hushed expectation. "I do not believe I am aware of the cause of this event."

"Fair enough," Charlotte sighed. "It was worth a try. Well, time to use the only method left to us: wake the dead. At least metaphorically...I hope. Although I don't relish pawing through the corpses of the other aviatrixes or their ship, I also don't want whatever grounded a ship of that size to get ahold of us. The *Harlot's Promise* is barely holding together structurally, and without our seaward fin we've got all the maneuverability of a bird frozen by a winter storm."

They dropped the boarding ramp, sending up a plume of choking dust as the end smacked onto the ground. The opening of the cavern's roof had dumped a few hundred pounds of dirt and scraggly plant life over the wreckage and landing spot, but most of the dust covering the ship's remains had been granted by time itself. The dusty plume from the ramp swirled for a moment before it was drawn to the ground as if a giant had sucked in his breath, an effect simple gravity could not accomplish.

"Electrostatic current," Charlotte guessed, confirming it with a device hanging from the tool belt that she'd fastened on. Whether generated by mystic or mundane means, the cavern had been designed to quickly take care of any dust or dirt that could drift into working gears.

"But that makes no damn sense," Charlotte muttered, shaking her head. "The power output required to maintain a field over a space of this size..."

A suspicion had taken root in the aviatrix's mind, but she was loathe to leap to such hasty conclusions. So lost in thought she was that Charlotte didn't notice Tash gliding down the gangplank to the dirt floor until the automaton was already lifting her skirt delicately to avoid getting the hem dirty.

Tash crouched down, skirts hiked up to keep them safe, brushing dirt away from an indentation that had caught her toe. The dust wanted to cling to the stone underneath, but the Doll wasn't taking "no" for an answer. There was an excitement to her movements, as if she'd discovered a piece of vital history.

"There are carvings on these floors," Tash said, tracing her fingers over them. "Religious significance is likely. Early Babylonian, perhaps late Sumerian. I would have to see more to know for certain. A winged leonine form, but with a scorpion's tail, has been stamped into the bricks as some sort of maker's mark."

Although the fae lights did what they could to fight back the gloom, it was just too large an area for the tiny glowing marbles to sufficiently light. The quartz lights on the *Harlot's Promise* also refused to blaze above a certain level, leaving the island of illumination in the area dim and ineffectual. The shadows around the ship had begun to take on a malevolent feel to them.

"Ancient Babylonians had retractable roofs and airships?" Charlotte asked sarcastically, the creeping dread on the cavern beginning to wear on the aviatrix and making her tone sharper than had been intended. "Fascinating all the stuff historians missed. How do you know all these things, Tash? No, no, stop. I've heard it before: your memories are shadows under the ice, and you don't get to choose what breaks through. But still. Sometimes I swear you mystery it up a bit much."

"Your frustration is understandable, Captain Frost," Tash responded, words as stiff as the wreckage of the airships, her face motionless. "Be assured that I, too, find the absence of my memories both inconvenient and irritating. Perhaps even more so than you."

"Wait, I didn't mean it like that," Charlotte objected, realizing she'd let her exasperation and fear boil over too much and was being churlish with her companion.

Tash did not answer, instead turning and striding away under the pretense of examining more floor carvings.

Charlotte felt like kicking herself in the head. But instead of attempting the acrobatically inadvisable feat, the aviatrix directed the fae lights into a closer orbit above her. Tash had no need of light with her mechanical senses, and the luminous spheres emitted enough glow so that Charlotte's immediate surroundings were fairly well-lit when the swarm contracted above. Of course, if there *was* a danger lurking in the darkness then she'd be a beacon for its attention, the brightest thing in the cavern. But the aviatrix had found that fear of the unknown was much worse than confronting the things that prowled the fringes.

Tash was still silent, petulantly choosing the carvings and pieces of crashed ship farthest away from the *Harlot's Promise* to investigate. Charlotte decided to give Tash the space she obviously wanted and headed for wreckage away from the pouting automaton. Unable to use her goggles, Charlotte was reduced to scanning the area with the hand-held aetherometer she'd used to confirm the current running through the floor. Although less intuitive and not as exact as the goggles, the tri-cylinder device was adept enough at detecting more powerful magics. The floor was charged with mystic force, but it was concentrated, and the normal bleed-off from the aura wasn't present. Instead, the aviatrix took note of how the aetherometer itself was losing power much faster than the scanning device should have, as if it was being drained by an outside source. To test her hypothesis, Charlotte directed one of the fae lights to approach the floor while carefully monitoring it. The glowing orb grew fainter as it dropped lower, showing a loss of energy that the aetherometer confirmed.

The moment the fae light touched the floor it was snuffed out as quickly as an ember doused by the rain. Charlotte could not reinitiate the magic link to the dead marble. It lay there forlorn and useless.

Dead.

Chapter 2

"Tash...Tash!"

"Yes?" the Doll replied to her shout. There was still a stiffness to her tone, but she'd picked up on the captain's alarmed state enough to not ignore the aviatrix.

"Get back on the *Harlot's Promise*! Now!"

An insulted harrumph from Tash was the opening salvo of an argument that had begun to brew, but Charlotte's panicked tone cut through it.

"Tash, get back on the damned ship! Please!"

The sheer terror in the aviatrix's voice was enough to make Tash hike up her ruffled skirts and sprint for the Liberty Ship. The automaton was within three steps of the ramp when her feet suddenly slowed and stumbled on each other. Surprised shock spread across Tash's alabaster face as she tumbled head over heels into the dirt of the cavern floor.

Abandoning all thoughts of caution Charlotte ran at full tilt for her companion, sliding down and hooking her arms under the courtesan's armpits. She pulled with all her strength, barely managing to get Tash to her feet again.

Tash's neck went stiff, and mewling sounds of panic came out of the Doll's suddenly frozen mouth.

Charlotte grunted and strained under the automaton's weight as she dragged Tash toward the boarding ramp. Normally the supernatural forces that animated and softened Tash's form would have also counteracted the weight of her golden mechanisms, but just as the Doll herself was becoming inert, so too were all her mystical subsystems failing. Combined with the death of the fae light that had dared touch the floor, it led to a single conclusion.

The cavern floor was draining magic away like a leech bleeding their host.

And just as the answer was inescapable, so too might the abandoned hangar prove to be as well.

Charlotte pulled energy from the batteries aboard the *Harlot's Promise* to reinforce her burning muscles, giving her a sudden burst of strength as she yanked Tash onto the ramp and pulled her up. The captain cut her personal power drain as soon as she could, but in that moment of contact her fears had been confirmed.

The ship's power stores were being siphoned off at an alarming rate.

"Great. Just fucking peachy," Charlotte grunted through clenched teeth as she dragged Tash up the ramp into the dubious safety of the ship. The batteries on the *Harlot's Promise* were already critically low, far below safe thresholds. She collapsed panting on the upper deck, the Doll's head cradled in her lap. Charlotte fought back frustration, shutting her eyes tight and willing the hot tears away. "The fun just keeps piling on. Even if we could open the roof again, we don't have the energy to get off the ground, let alone run from whoever gets sent after us."

Sculpted alabaster fingers, cold and stiff, stroked the back of Charlotte's neck. Her eyes flew open in surprise to see Tash's gaze locked on her face. A single tear has escaped the aviatrix's iron will to splash on the Doll's cheek. But where before it would have softly landed as if on warm skin, this tear splashed off the white skin like water off hard porcelain.

"My...beautiful mistress...," Tash whispered, her lips barely moving.

Icy dread gripped Charlotte's stomach like a clenched fist, sickening her with grief she struggled to keep under control.

"Stop that," Charlotte admonished her companion gently. Another tear escaped her control, splashing on the golden lips that struggled to form words. Tash was trying to say something, perhaps to warn her, or to declare the undying devotion the strange machine woman had shown the captain since their escape from Godmother. "Save your strength, Tash. There's some form of suppression field draining the magic in the cavern. All I have to do is find the source, deactivate it, and voila, you'll be good as new."

Tash gave no sign of hearing her, and as Charlotte stroked the frozen face of the Doll the light faded from the featureless golden eyes, leaving naught but dead auric orbs staring out in the distance. Her arm was still hooked around the captain's neck, but Tash had used the last of her strength to loosen her grip so that the aviatrix could easily free herself.

"Wake up, Tash," Charlotte found herself crying, feeling the fool even as she heard the words issue forth. "You can go back to being mad at me. Just move, speak, anything…"

Only silence answered her.

Charlotte shook her head, angry at herself, wiping her tears away with her scarlet leather sleeve.

"That's enough of that," she sternly told herself. "The more time you waste blubbering, the less chance that Tash has. Pull it together, damn you!"

Carefully disentangling herself from the inert Doll, Charlotte got to her feet. The fae lights that had dimmed with her emotions blazed brighter as she calmed her breathing. As if in defiance of the gods, the captain stalked down the gangplank, anger keeping her fear at bay.

"You think that shit's going to work on me?" Charlotte growled, kicking the sand on the cavern floor. The grains clung tenaciously to the static field covering the floor, and the aviatrix nearly broke her toe trying to dislodge the stubborn dust from its bed.

"That all you got?" she yelled out into the void, her voice strangely muted in the massive cavern. "You can't deactivate *me* so easy! You'd better be an automated system, because if you're not, whoever you are, whatever you are, I'm going to drag your ass out here and beat the stupid out of you!"

Nothing, not even echoes, answered her in the dark cavern.

"Yeah, you tell them, loon," Charlotte grunted,

cracking a wry smile at her grandiose outburst. "I'm sure the dirt is shaking in its boots."

Briefly the aviatrix considered channeling more energy into Tash; the earlier kiss had unintentionally siphoned off some of Charlotte's magic, restoring the Doll for a brief time. But there was no telling how the leeching field was affecting Charlotte's own powers. Although she appeared to be resistant to the suppression field for the time being, there was no reason to assume that she was immune to the eventual ill effects.

The fae lights spun around the aviatrix, flitting off at her whispered command to illuminate the nearby wreckage of the larger airship. Although it was impossible the old craft had any magic left in its batteries, the scattering of the debris indicated the *Lilith's Embrace* hadn't fallen from lack of power.

Someone had crashed it at full throttle into the ground.

Charlotte ticked off the ship's scattered parts methodically in her head, rebuilding it in her imagination. From its crude design it was obviously a first-generation Matriarchy craft, lacking the efficiency of elegance that graced the *Harlot's Promise* and her sister ships. The first aviatrixes hadn't cared as much for the style of their escape vessels so much as their functionality. The years of floating beyond the reach of the normal world had brought a decadent beauty to the engineering of the Liberty Ships, utilizing the mystic forces to create craft of sweeping grandeur. There was a brutal honesty to the basic design of the *Lilith's Embrace* that spoke of the rebellious hopes of her creators. The hands that had fashioned the ship were used to being struck, denied, broken. That the airship existed at all was a testament to the strength of those who had dared to dream of more.

But something was off.

There were parts that didn't belong, shapes that weren't right, alien and smooth compared to the angular simplicity of the Matriarchy's work. The fairy lights zoomed closer, hovering over a mass of tangled wreckage that belonged to neither ship nor floor.

The dead aviatrixes hadn't just decided to nose their ship into the ground on a whim. There'd been something else present, a construct of some kind.

They'd crashed the *Lilith's Embrace* into that something to kill it.

Like a spider under a boot, Charlotte could piece together a very rough idea of what the foreign automaton had looked like. In size it had been equivalent to a small horse or cow, comprised of flowing interconnecting armored plates. A long section of what could only be described as a monstrous scorpion tail lay lifeless behind the four-legged machine, its carapace mostly intact. There were scattered gears and hydraulics around the impact site, far too delicate in design to be any airship's internal machinery. Dust blanketed the destroyed construct, but the fae light glinted off areas that had been disturbed by their landing. Leaning down and picking a gear out of the wreckage, Charlotte was surprised by its heavy weight. Bereft of the static field of the cavern floor, the dry sand brushed off easily. Charlotte realized with a cold chill why the errant component was so heavy.

It was made of a gold alloy that she had only recently encountered in one other automaton.

Confused, Charlotte dusted off one of the main plates of the mystery machine crushed under the airship, using a trickle of personal magic to counteract the static effect. Her heart caught in her throat as bone-white ivory shone from her efforts, the inlaid silver lines of the armored plates as hauntingly familiar as the golden gear in her hand. The automaton's shape was that of a fantastical beast, comically oversized, but there was no doubt in the aviatrix's mind now.

The same artisan that had unleased this monstrosity into the world had also crafted Tash.

The design elements, the craftsmanship of the pieces in delicacy intermixed with function, they were beyond anything that any tantric engineer alive was capable of. Malevolence seeped from the darkness beyond the fae lights, clinging to the destroyed ship and the horrific Doll-thing. Charlotte imagined she could hear things skittering at the edge of the fae lights' radius, their cold eyes tracking her every move. Goosebumps crawled up her arms, making her shiver as if a cold wind had blown over her grave.

Berating herself silently for her fears, the aviatrix sent the hovering lights into a wide radius. Although their glow was nearly swallowed by the dark, they provided just enough light that she could see a walkway around the perimeter of the cavern, connecting multiple platforms with tools and parts on them. Despite the cruder materials it was constructed from the scaffolding was much like the docking and repair decks that ringed the Matriarchy's flying city. It was easy to see that while this was the *Lilith's Embrace* origination point that there had been other ships that shared its berth. Given the scale of the operation, Charlotte was willing to bet that significant portions of Godmother had been built here as well before being integrated into the Amethyst City.

The crew of the downed ship had sacrificed themselves to save their sister engineers and the dream of the future.

But what of the monster destroyed by the *Lilith's Embrace*? Although it bore some semblance to the tantrically-animated creations of the Matriarchy it was clearly crafted by no aviatrix, nor was it an ally of the sisterhood. Just like Tash. Only significantly more disturbing. What was it? Where had it come from? And perhaps most importantly...

Were there more of them lurking around the cavern?

The fear that had been held at bay by force of will came in fast and sharp, a blade in the night, cutting into the captain's heart like an icy dagger. Despite herself, Charlotte couldn't keep from reconstructing the alien automaton in her mind, a part of her marveling at the ridiculously terrifying artistry that would have gone into such a monster. The beating of the aviatrix's heart was loud in her ears, muffling the world, and she could feel the panic slithering in like a serpent through the back door. Charlotte clenched her fists, willing the fear back and forcing her spine straight, refusing to give in to panic. Sometimes she hated how easily her mind could fit together broken machinery into a functional image. Normally it was an incredible advantage in the Art.

But not this time.

"So, this was a demonic scorpion-thing the size of a horse. Nope. Didn't want to imagine that. Bad brain. Soon as we make a proper port, I'm poisoning you with the worst whiskey I can find."

Talking to herself was just one of the strange habits she'd acquired in the months since her marriage had ended. And although she found herself to be rather predictable company, it did help to hear a voice in the dark depths, even if it was her own and quavering with fear.

"Focus on the job, Frost," she chided herself. "Tash is relying on you. And if this floor is draining magic, how long until it siphons you dry as well?"

Swallowing her disgust, Charlotte recalled the fae lights to hover above her, emitting a kaleidoscope of colors. The glow from the tiny marbles flowed over the pieces of the crushed monster sticking out from under the *Lilith's Embrace*. The aviatrix was loath to study the one section that had been left intact by the collision, but there was precious little information to be gleaned from the squashed bug bits.

"But you," she said with a heavy sigh, looking at the nearly undamaged scorpion tail frozen in a curled strike aimed at the ship that had killed it. "You just had to be the bit to survive, didn't you? Asshole."

She giggled at the fact it likely *was* the mechanical rectum of the creature. There was a manic edge to the giggle, and the aviatrix took a moment to steady herself with pranayama breathing.

"It's more like a lobster tail than a scorpion's," Charlotte told herself. "Even though it curls around like a stinger. Those bits on the end? Not venomous barbs. They don't even look like they could pierce flesh...unless thrust forward with sufficient velocity that is."

A rush of anger made her cheeks burn.

"I'm warning you, woman. That's enough of that," Charlotte said sternly, resisting the urge to headbutt a girder to show her brain who was boss. "Godmother raised me better than this; I am *not* a mewling lady at the ball who broke a nail. Let the grounders run screaming from the unknown; I am a goddamn Liberty Captain and a tantric engineer. Fuck it or kill it, either way, nothing stops me."

Her heartbeat slowed, and a very irritated Charlotte Frost turned suspicious attention inward.

Deep in the mystic veins of her body she saw the same malignant spell that had drained Tash of her magic working away at the aviatrix's own stores like a rat at the grain, burrowing deeper, bleeding her out aetherically. With a start, she realized that the corrosive decay was also affecting her emotions.

Relief broke through like floodwaters cracking a dam. True, there wasn't much she could do to stop the negative effects of the suppression field. But knowing that the cavern was the root of her sudden bout of nerves allowed Charlotte's mind to settle, content in the knowledge that she wasn't losing her mind or, worse yet, her courage.

Charlotte's hands were steady and sure as she reached out to run her fingers along the ivory monster's tail. Although segmented like an insect's, the sections melded together so precisely that it was virtually impossible to find the seams. Although the innards were easily visible where it had burst from the ship's impact, Charlotte felt a burning curiosity to see the actual workings undisturbed, rather than as junk scattered from the deathblow. But to do that she had to find a place, a specific spot in the carapace…

"Ha!" the aviatrix exclaimed with triumph. "Got you."

The strange alloy of the shell had been warped ever so slightly, a chink in the armor that her fingertips nearly missed. Charlotte pulled her heaviest screwdriver off her belt along with a rubber shaping mallet and prayed the steel of the tool would hold. With small taps, careful of the angle to not stress the screwdriver too much, she slowly hammered it into the fissure she'd discovered.

A small bit of the carapace screeched up, and the aviatrix was surprised to find it was wafer-thin.

She gave a low whistle of appreciation. Monster or not, a true artisan had crafted the automaton. "All the strength of the libidium-infused steel the Matriarchy uses, at a fraction of the thickness. In fact, if I didn't know better, I'd swear it was actual ivory. But I've never seen anything from the East of sufficient volume to craft even one of the armor plates on this thing, let alone the whole—"

Charlotte was interrupted by a spark from the mechanical tail as her screwdriver touched the gears inside, sending a jolt of magic up her arm like a lightning bolt. She fell back with a cry, releasing the leather-handled screwdriver as amethyst sparks lit the steel of the tool from the inside out. The abandoned screwdriver fell out of the monster's tail frame, blackened and twisted by its misadventure. Charlotte gave a low whistle as she toed the scorched screwdriver with her work boot.

"Okay. Obviously not my brightest idea. I'd thought the leeching field would have drained this bug dry. Maybe I breached a protected node, or just plain stabbed a battery. Still, with a prybar from the ship and sufficient precautions…"

Tash's silent form seemed to stare at her in apprehension.

"Yeah, yeah," Charlotte muttered to the inert automaton. "I can feel your judging look even now. Still, maybe my subconscious is trying to keep me from getting killed by imagining your disappointment. The decay rate on my magic isn't as strong as what happened to you, Tash; organics seem harder to bleed dry than mechanicals. And if I did break open a battery in this scorpion's shell, it needs time to drain the remnant magic away. Either way, perhaps a less hasty decision is in order."

Leaving her static companion by the wreckage of monster and ship, Charlotte picked her way to the nearest wall of the cavern, her footsteps light and furtive. She didn't want any more surprises. Without Tash she had no backup, and if she triggered a trap of some kind that'd be the end of both of them.

The fae lights were noticeably dimmer now, but Charlotte was loath to push more energy into the floating marbles. There was no telling what form the switch to turn off the suppression field would take, even if she were able to find it. There was every reason to believe she'd have to energize the "off" switch with her own mystic arts. Magic, a rare and valuable commodity to begin with, had become more precious in the depth of the ruined temple of Ishtar.

Blue glazing reflected the light of the orbs through patches in the centuries-old dirt covering the wall, flickering back at the fae lights as if encouraging them to shine brighter. From what little Charlotte knew of the building techniques of the region it was precisely what one would expect to find in an abandoned holy place.

Charlotte pulled a spectrum perceptor out of a hard leather pouch on her belt, its delicate form wrapped in soft felt. It resembled a jeweler's loupe, with a protruding eyepiece set with multiple tiny lenses of treated glass within its copper housing. The perceptor was fitted with a diagonal leather head strap, a trick that clockmakers had used for centuries to free their hands for delicate work. The aviatrix slipped it on and took a closer look at the wall. There had to be something else, something unique about this place. The aviatrixes of old had launched from here for a reason. It was impossible that the first actual magicians the world had seen in several millennia had just happened to set up base beneath Arslan Tash. The mechanisms of the entry slabs were as ancient as the carvings, and her companion's very existence gave lie to any claim of coincidence with the ruins.

Fortunately, the perceptor was only able to detect the most basic of mystic currents; its primary function was to provide a composition reading that someone who'd been trained in the Art could interpret. But the kaleidoscope of color it revealed was still too bright, the walls pulsing with magic. Fortunately, the monocle had been designed for much finer work than the goggles, simultaneously allowing her to tune down the magic the Arslan Tash ruins were bathed in while enhancing the more mundane aspects of the world.

"Sandstone bricks...bitumen mortar..." Charlotte murmured, identifying the mineral colors that pulsed at the periphery of the perceptor as she squinted at the wall. The bricks were about a foot and half across, with a couple of inches of mortar joining them to their neighbors.

She reached out and ran her fingers over the blue glaze. It was pockmarked by age, a protective coating that had preserved the sandstone behind it with remarkable efficacy. Tiny crystal flakes embedded in the glazing reflected the fae lights. Charlotte didn't need the perceptor to tell her this was the source of the mystic forces running through the temple. She gave a low whistle of appreciation.

The ancient Temple of Ishtar was an oversized tantric battery.

"I wonder how many came to the temple of the goddess of love...how many sexual liaisons, how many orgies, were conducted above," Charlotte whispered. "Did they know you were draining their energies? Did it make you come harder?"

Untold centuries of sexual rites dedicated to Ishtar had been performed above the hidden complex. The temple itself acted as a giant receiver, and the charged crystal flakes in the walls dutifully held on to the energy in defiance of natural entropic laws. Given the amount of magic she'd detected on the way in, it was obvious that the blue glazing must run through most, if not all, of the ruins. It chilled the captain's bones to think of that amount of accumulated magic falling into the wrong hands.

There were further decorations embedded in the glaze, an imprint that mirrored the sculpts on the floor. The maned lions stamped into each brick had been beautifully gilded once, but now all the was left of the thin gold leafing were scattered flakes hanging on for dear life. The walls didn't share the same electrostatic current as the floor, so dust hadn't found easy purchase on them. Although the years had not been kind to the lion decorations, after examining several Charlotte discovered that universally something was wrong with them. What at first she'd assumed to be the damage of time was an intended effect. The bodies of the "lions" were thicker and lower to the ground, but that wasn't what caught her attention. Their tails were far too thick and long, curving back around to loom menacingly over their bodies in every single one.

Like scorpions.

Dread and excitement both warred within her guts. Although it was impossible to tell what the monster Doll's head had looked like now, Charlotte had a sneaking suspicion she knew what lay buried under a half ton of wreckage in the cavern.

"Keep your eyes peeled for lion-scorpions," the aviatrix called over her shoulder to the motionless Tash. The automaton's blank gold eyes gave no sign of comprehension. "What do we call them? They can't be the manticores from Greek mythology, as that is clearly a leonine head, not a human one. Is there another word for that? Lorpions? Scorlions?"

Silence.

"You're right," Charlotte said, trying to not panic at the

absent state of her companion's mind. "Until we figure it out, manticore is a lot easier to remember, and you can use it in polite conversation without sounding like a loon. Mostly."

The silence of her motionless companion refocused Charlotte's attention back on the mystic elements of the wall. The Matriarchy claimed that their tantric Art was descended from older techniques, but the aviatrix had met many a charlatan on the ground that made the same boast about the origins of their secret cults. This one claimed descent from the Templars, that one from the Gnostic Christians, and so forth, all with their little folklore stories that they would somehow grant them legitimacy above other occultists. It was just a smokescreen to hide the fact that they'd stolen or "borrowed" huge sections of their teachings from elsewhere and manipulated it to suit their needs. Each had been an illusion, falsified spiritual powers and promises to bilk the ignorant out of their money.

But this was different. Tantric magic worked; the *Harlot's Promise* was a solid example of that, as was Godmother and the entire Legion of Lilith. Charlotte had assumed the Crones' claims that the Art extended back millennia had been a useful fiction, a story that would keep the complacent under thumb and satisfied without prying too deep. Charlotte hadn't cared much about the origins of their mystic enhancements of gears and springs; it worked, and that was enough for her. No matter who claimed discovery, the physical laws of the universe waited, uncaring of the names of those who sought them.

Lauren, her ex-wife, had been considerably less

pragmatic about the Art, and it had fueled her infatuation with the past, a passion that led to discovering the myth of leylines written in ancient texts. Supposedly, mystical lines of force crisscrossed the planet in an arcane network of power that could be tapped into. But in all her travels, Charlotte had never been able to identify such a grid to the magic; the land had a universal constant level of energy more reliant on population count than anything inherently special about the location. Lauren had insisted that ancient peoples had been able to access the mythical leylines to fuel their own magics; she'd theorized the rise of the Matriarchy's tantric magic had coincided with a pulse of energy that had broken the leylines as a river breaks the dam after a flood.

But by that thought the magic should have been available for anyone with the will and rituals to access it. That only aviatrixes could use it through tantric engineering had reinforced their beliefs in the justness of their cause and ways, giving rise to some crediting the ancient rebel goddess Lilith with blessing them. Although the magic was aspected by sex and produced by it, it shouldn't have made any difference in who used it and how. Energy was energy at the fundamental level. Magic was directed adaptation, controlled chaos, and just as any manner of pipe could conduct water so too should have the hoary old crafts been able to manipulate the mystical energies of the world. Lauren's theories had been rejected out of hand by the Crone Council, who'd rightly pointed out that if that her premise was true, that magic was not their sole purview, then why hadn't practioners from other Arts appeared?

This place, this temple, its design and materials were ancient, lending the weight of millennia to the Crones' argument. But why tantric magic? Why not the gnostic practices of the English ritualists, or any other set of cultists who had attempted to manipulate the underlying weave of reality?

There was no doubt that the first aviatrixes two decades ago had not built this place. It was obvious they'd merely utilized it, and Charlotte was eager to find out if there were more secrets the cavern held that the Matriarchy had tried to bury. The age of the blue energy-trapping glaze, the bricks protected by it, the strange manticore-like creature embossed on each of them, all of it led to one inescapable conclusion.

The ancient Syrians had been practioners of the tantric Art.

The well-preserved walls proved that magic was not the sole dominion of the Matriarchy. The figures depicted in all manners of erotic exercise were not only female, but also male, both, and all variations of nature.

The perceptor picked up a subtle imprinted pattern in the brickwork, a familiar shape that made Charlotte's breath catch. The indentation would have been easy to miss even in full light if you didn't know to look for it; only the differences in the spectral signature allowed the aviatrix to see it so clearly. The aviatrix pulled off her gloves and ran her bare fingertips over the glazed stone, feeling the pits and shallows and valleys that were easy to miss with the naked eye. Whoever had protected the wall with the coating had been careful to not let it pool in the subtle crevices of what was carved into the stone, so that by touch Charlotte was able to confirm what the perceptor had revealed.

A luscious woman had been carved in the brickwork of the wall, hidden so that only touch could find it.

Someone had gone to considerable trouble to make the unseen woman as accurate as possible, and the aviatrix gave a naughty smile as her hands ran up the thigh of the carving. The sculptor had been lovingly precise with the vagina. Charlotte idly stroked a finger over the immaculately carved clit of the artwork, marveling at how the hood almost seemed to move under her finger.

A sudden click within the wall made Charlotte jump back with a startled gasp. It hadn't been her imagination; the hood *had* moved, and there had been an actual button within.

Dust puffed out as giant gears ground behind the glazed stone, and the mortar around the bricks of the carving split into seams. The aviatrix stepped back, expecting the entire section of wall to suddenly start moving. She grinned at the thought of someone hiding such a simple button in an overlooked place that no virginal zealot or sanctimonious imbecile would look for.

A small panel puffed open, the thin stone plate sliding back a disappointment of a finale for all the grinding gear sounds.

The revealed indentation was only about a foot across in diameter, and an inch deep. Strange holes were spaced at irregular intervals around the hollow.

"It's a socket," Charlotte murmured to herself, fingers lightly dancing over the odd holes, tracing shape and depth.

Her mind was alighting with possibilities as her gaze turned back toward the crushed manticore.

The strange amalgamation of rods and shapes at the end of its scorpion tail looked like it just might fit.

"Okay, big boy," she said with a grin as her hands went to her toolbelt. "Let's put your ass to work."

Chapter 3

"Damn it, open up!" Charlotte grunted with exasperation, putting all her weight behind the giant wrench.

The recalcitrant metal plate finally gave way with a surly screech as it fell away from the manticore's frame.

Within the crushed automaton was a dizzying array of tiny golden gears, screws, springs, and other bits. Charlotte huffed her breath out in irritation.

"Couldn't just make this simple, could you?" she complained to the lifeless machine as she studied the insides with the perceptor monocle. "You're just as complicated as your inert sister. Both sleeping beauties, just snoozing the time away."

The cavern echoed hollowly with her cackle, and Charlotte wished for the thousandth time that Tash was active and flirting with her. Or talking. Or just being there. The lonely aviatrix had accepted her isolation for the choices she'd made since the divorce, the stand she took against Lauren's lies, but she'd gotten used to the clockwork courtesan's presence quickly over the last couple of days.

"No, not *used* to her," Charlotte corrected herself aloud.

"I miss Tash. Be specific. She's got me smitten. I crave those flirtations, those secret whispers that make my skin tingle. And she was excellent at oral. Be honest with yourself, Frost."

Satisfied that her mind was sufficiently chastised, the aviatrix returned to her work.

Charlotte had managed to use the damage inflicted by the crashed *Lilith's Embrace* to detach the rear of the machine crushed beneath, but the monster automaton's tail was still far too large and heavy to drag over to the wall panel. The aviatrix was sure her back would give out before she even got it that far, let alone be able to manipulate the end of the tail into the lock.

Fortunately, despite its strange craftsmanship, many of the gear configurations and components within the tail were like those in the Matriarchy's automatons. Although much of the manticore's internal functions remained a mystery to the aviatrix, Charlotte was able to understand enough to jury-rig something functional. Letting her hands move in accord with the nearly subconscious pattern recognition, the aviatrix pried deeper into the tail with screwdriver and hammer, chisel and pliers. She'd identified early on what she assumed was the battery component her screwdriver had penetrated before and had disconnected it from the rest of the machinery; so far, she hadn't electrocuted herself with all her tinkering, so that was a good sign.

"You'll need legs," she muttered, her hands stripping down the hydraulics that connected the tail to the main body, releasing it with a thud as it hit the ground. "These will do, with a few modifications."

After a couple of hours of hard work, a form began to take shape from the wrecked monster. The former tail was in shape now like a shrimp, a thick front that narrowed into the section of the tail that still held the key configuration for the panel. Six spindly golden legs jutted out, three to each side, the repurposed golden innards of the destroyed parent machine. The legs twitched in the fae light as if dreading the bulk they were supposed to bear. Charlotte had to keep reminding herself that the metal was an alloy she hadn't encountered before, not pure gold, and so could support the weight of the machinery. At least she hoped it would.

"Let's see...there's something missing..." Charlotte murmured. "Ah, of course!"

To pilot the tail-thing to the panel, the aviatrix would have to subsume part of her mind into the frame, much as she did with the *Harlot's Promise*. Without a sensing apparatus she'd bump both it and her into the wall and never find the target.

Her creature needed eyes.

Charlotte waved her hand in the air, extending a thread of magic into the air that recalled the swarm of artificial fairies lighting the area. Bereft of directed control they'd drifted away a bit, but the call from their mistress caused them to flare bright and streak back to her. She smiled in loving pride at their obedience, taking a moment to spin them around her like frisky constellations of tiny stars.

Turning back to the manticore's modified tail she twirled her fingers and sent the crystals into the front hollow where it had connected to its parent monster. The fae settled into place, and the new automaton welcomed their presence as tiny gearwork shifted and connected to the libidium-infused quartz, providing a rudimentary system of sight. Warily she reconnected what she assumed were the internal batteries, ready to jump back if she accidentally shocked herself again. There was no guarantee that she had not made some critical error with the foreign components, and in matters of both machines and magic such mistakes could lead to the same explosive result.

The legs twitched as she slid a part into place, a disturbing sign of life that was nonetheless what she was hoping for. She'd been feeding a steady trickle of her own magic into the machine as she modified it, recharging the battery as she worked. Although she had held back a couple of the fae lights to illuminate the area, the shadows were thick and deep around the cavern from the diminished light, and the aviatrix could feel the exhausted drain of the suppression field sapping her. It would be easy to begin imagining things moving in the darkness, creatures of flesh and steel awakened from their slumber, creeping up on the intruders, closer, their breath on her neck...

"Ouch!" the aviatrix exclaimed as one of the golden gears snapped into place and began to whir. She hadn't quite been fast enough, and the moving part had caught a finger and drawn a drop of blood. Her heart fluttered with fear. "Even with the battery connected you shouldn't be moving yet. I haven't initiated a link with you."

A shudder ran through the machine, and other springs and gears moved together of their own accord, as if magnetically attracted. Parts snapped into place where they were supposed to go, with no help from her. Thoughts of ghosts and possession sent a cold sliver of dread through Charlotte, but she quickly dismissed such juvenile notions, chastising herself for such flights of fancy. Just because magic existed did not mean that every child's fevered dream had been given life in the world.

There was glittering movement across the golden innards that at first Charlotte mistook as a trick of the dim light. But the way it gave the illusion of movement made her suspicious, and she peered as close as she could at the parts with the perceptor at maximum magnification.

Grains of sand had gotten into the gears.

"But dust doesn't move without wind," Charlotte muttered, reaching a gloved fingertip out to the glittering grains.

They moved away as if startled by her poke.

"What the hell are you?" she breathed, watching as the "sand" reformed itself into a line of movement, like ants marching back home.

Another shudder rattled the automaton. The aviatrix pulled her hands completely free as the parts began moving of their own accord, rearranging, and settling into each other. The grains of not-sand skittered away as machinery locked into new formations. Charlotte raised her heavy wrench in startled fear as the segmented ivory shell of the manticore's modified tail closed in, sealing itself. Lights flickered within the fae marbles like the eyes of a spider at twilight. The golden legs twitched with purpose, gathering under the machine, steadying it. The automaton rose to the height of a medium-sized dog, its width narrowing from the makeshift head to the end of the twitching tail and its array of protrusions.

The tangled conglomeration of machinery that comprised the automaton's head sank within the segmented ivory shell a few inches, like a turtle pulling into its shell, and the fae eyes blazed brighter. Within the shadowed overhang of the carapace, it was as if a galaxy had ignited, twinkling stars suspended in the gloom of limitless night. The reborn automaton stretched its segmented body and legs like a cat awakening from a nap before shaking itself as if fresh from a bath. The crystal eyes peered up at Charlotte quizzically.

She sensed no menace from the machine, only curiosity.

"Um. Huh. Welcome to life?" the aviatrix said, not quite sure what to make of the thing's behavior. She had expected to have to struggle to get the machine into position even with her repairs; that it had taken over her modification efforts and restored itself to a mobile automaton was both fascinating and disturbing. The aviatrix hadn't installed anything even close to a mind, and the appearance of one had taken her aback.

The automaton's fae eyes shone brighter, swaying its small scorpion tail cautiously. The machine took a couple of hesitant steps toward Charlotte. She realized she was still holding the heavy wrench as if about to strike the construct and lowered it with a comforting smile.

"It's okay, sugar," she said in a soothing tone. "I'm not going to hurt you."

The crystals burned brighter, shifting into a comforted

blue tone, and the machine skittered closer with more confidence. Charlotte fought to not cringe back as the ivory-shelled thing pressed in against her leg, as if seeking comfort. The aviatrix braced for the impact, but there was barely a whisper of weight against her leg. Warmth emanated from its frame, although the animating magic had not softened its shell.

"How are you doing that?" she asked in wonderment. "With that much gold alloy and plating you should be at least a hundred pounds, if not more."

As if in answer the automaton jumped into her arms.

Charlotte cried out, expecting to be knocked down by the eager machine. But when she reflexively caught the automaton, she was surprised by how light it was. The perceptor monocle detected a faint but familiar aura around the shell of the rebuilt manticore.

"Ha!" the aviatrix said with a smile. "You're using a variation of the same gravity-negating technology as the Liberty Ships have. Or, given the age and looks of this place, it might be more accurate to say we use the same system as you. I'd bet dollars to dumplings that they pirated your systems for our craft. Are you manipulating your crystal core to generate an anti-gravity field or is your frame an alloy like libidium?"

The automaton stared up at her, a strange sort of innocence in its crystal eyes. A complicated series of colors flashed over their eyes, an attempt at an answer. It made the aviatrix feel like a dunce that she had no idea what the machine was trying to communicate.

"Just how intelligent are you, anyway?" Charlotte

murmured. "Can you comprehend my speech and intentions? Are you more like a dog or a human? What level of sentience do you have? Are you an 'it' or...something else?"

Crystal eyes flared as scarlet as the aviatrix's flight leathers and the machine leapt out of her arms as nimbly as they had jumped into them. Irritation was clear in the movements as they lashed their scorpion tail back and forth. Charlotte held up her hands to placate the new lifeform.

"Okay, well, that answers that," she said, lightening her tone. "Not an 'it,' then. Sorry if I offended you. That you can be angered by my words tells me quite a bit about how smart you are. But what I don't understand is how? Don't take this the wrong way, but where did your mind come from?"

The mechanical scorpion cocked their tail quizzically, scarlet face-lights dimming back to a neutral white.

"You, um, you don't have a proper head," Charlotte explained, careful to keep her tone friendly. "Even Tash, the most advanced Doll I've ever encountered, has a head and, presumably, the calculation engine within that provides her with a control system. Although you seem to have an actual mind like her, I'm frankly flummoxed about where the hell you store it. I might not have an exact idea of what all your parts are or what they do, but there's no way I overlooked a cortex capable of housing an intelligence."

Crystal lights turned a deep green, and the automaton's frame shook as if a tiny earthquake had gripped them. Their legs tapped the floor in a random staccato, and Charlotte realized something surprising.

The scorpion was laughing at her.

"You don't want to do that, sugar," Charlotte warned, her tone darkening. Although it was irrational to feel as insulted as she did, she'd been on the outside looking in enough to know the sting of derision all too well.

Green lights shifted to turquoise then blue, and the modified automaton bowed their legs, bobbing their frame in acknowledgement. They straightened and, keeping their crystals glowing blue, scuttled back to her. One single golden insect leg extended toward her and stopped. Taking the proffered leg for an invitation, Charlotte leaned over adjusting the perceptor monocle.

Tiny glittering grains moved in a line along the leg before disappearing beneath a seam in the carapace,

"The sand in your gears," Charlotte breathed in astonishment. "It wasn't a hallucination, then. It was moving, infiltrating your frame? But that still doesn't make any sense..."

The automaton waited patiently, unmoving.

"Unless...of course! But no, that can't be. You *are* the sand?"

Excited chittering from inside the segmented body of the automaton and tiny taps of their legs on the floor combined with bright blue fae light seemed to confirm her suspicion.

Charlotte looked around nervously. It was some form of distributed intelligence, likely a hive mind. But that begged the question: was all the sentient sand inside the automaton? Or were there still grains lurking, ready to try and infect her skin and senses? There was no way to tell the common dirt and dust from the strange lifeform.

"The electrostatic field running through the floor," Charlotte murmured, a strange mixture of horror and admiration overtaking her. "It wasn't used to keep the sand out of machinery; it was used to capture *you*."

The scorpion chittered with excitement. They started toward Charlotte, but the aviatrix reflexively took a step back. There was a warble of concern from the automaton.

"Stop being stupid, Frost," the aviatrix chastised herself. "The scorpion hasn't been aggressive, even when you insulted it. Besides, if they had either the capacity or the desire to infiltrate your skin they wouldn't have waited until you literally built a body for them. They've had plenty of time to make you regret life before now.

"So, what do I call you, then?" the aviatrix asked the concerned scorpion, fighting back a nervous giggle. "Sandy?"

Although there was no breathing coming from the automaton, Charlotte could have sworn that she heard a huff of irritation. The modified machine turned and blazed their crystal eyes bright, spotlighting a section of the floor. The dust shifted sluggishly, clearing away from the floor in a pattern of Arabic letters. The curves and lines were beautiful, but incomprehensible to Charlotte. After a moment of her uncomfortably shrugging her shoulders, the scorpion shook its body as if heaving a beleaguered sigh. The sand shifted again, slower than before and with obvious effort from the automaton, into English letters.

"Shamhat," Charlotte read. The letters began to

disappear again as the static field pulled the sand flat and even again. The fae lights were a bit dimmer inside the scorpion's recessed head area, as if it had taken an extraordinary amount of effort. "That's what you prefer?"

The fae lights brightened blue, and Shamhat nodded their head.

"The electrostatic field is draining you, keeping you trapped," Charlotte muttered, hand to chin in thought. "Just like the leeching field is rendering Tash and the *Harlot's Promise* inert. It's all the same thing, isn't it? An artificial dead zone that no tantric technology works within?"

Shamhat's eyes turned neutral white then flashed bright blue once more.

"Is there a way to deactivate it?"

The automaton tapped its legs with excitement and leapt at the aviatrix.

Charlotte gave a startled scream and stepped back, reflexively swinging the heavy wrench at the attacking machine. The ill-aimed shot did nothing to deter Shamhat, instead serving as a platform for the lightweight automaton to scamper onto the aviatrix. Charlotte turned to protect her face, dropping the wrench, and trying to pry Shamhat off as they skittered around to her back.

"What the hell?!" Charlotte yelled, her flailing hands finally finding purchase on the shell of the machine.

Shamhat instantly froze in place. The fae lights over her shoulder flashed an inquisitive green, but the arms did not let go. Despite the seemingly low mass of the machine, the aviatrix was unable to pry the arms away that had clutched to her torso.

"Get the fuck off of me!" Charlotte growled, looking around for the wrench to add emphasis to her words.

Before she could lift the heavy tool off the floor though Shamhat sprang off nimbly, skittering back away from the enraged aviatrix with deep green lights.

"Lilith's tit, what the fuck was that all about?" Charlotte asked, her pulse racing in controlled panic from Shamhat's sudden aggressive actions.

Shamhat scuttled over to the panel the aviatrix had revealed in the wall. Looking back to make sure that Charlotte was watching, the machine extended up to its full height and curled its scorpion tail over the depressions in the panel. Shamhat's fae lights turned to an irritated orange as it inserted the tool-end of its tail into the lock.

Nothing happened.

As if to emphasize why they were annoyed, Shamhat stabbed their tail into the unrelenting lock a few more times, all to the same effect: nothing.

Charlotte's own annoyance rose in response. "Okay, but what do you want *me* to do about it? I don't have any parts that fit in there."

Shamhat shuddered in obvious irritation, the orange flashing closer to red. They skittered back toward Charlotte carefully, the fae lights fading from annoyance to a fuchsia then light purple, verging on pink. The aviatrix didn't understand what the machine was trying to communicate but allowed the hesitant Shamhat to reach forward a single gilded insect leg and touch her calf. With a sudden jerk, the tip of the leg pierced her red leather pants and into the skin underneath.

Tangled images of Tash, Lauren, and a host of other lovers flashed through Charlotte's mind. Her nipples hardened against her flight leathers as memories of lovemaking gone by blinked through the aviatrix's imagination. She closed her eyes for a moment, savoring the good times, ignoring the past pain that normally tainted such memories.

Shamhat withdrew their spider arm, and the sensations faded.

"Great, now I'm horny and Tash is still deactivated. Thanks for that," Charlotte said with a grouchy edge. Grudgingly, she had to admit that it provided ample evidence of one thing: the small automaton had the same sexual venom that Tash had been imbued with. It raised a whole host of unsettling questions and thoughts the aviatrix did not want to dwell on.

The automaton tapped its foreleg to get her to pay attention and pointed at one of the remaining fae lights that had been circling their location and providing light.

It had dimmed to almost nothing and drifted down to the floor.

Slowly, deliberately, Shamhat pointed at themself as well as the inert Tash before finally pointing back at the panel.

Charlotte felt like an idiot.

Shamhat didn't have the power to activate the switch on the wall. The tantric energy she'd managed to restore to the small automaton was already fading, being drained by the same dampening field that had shut down Tash and the *Harlot's Promise*. And there was only one way to restore it to any appreciable level.

"Are you implying what I hope you're not implying?" Charlotte asked the mechanical scorpion with shocked disbelief. "I don't know how to tell you this, sugar, but you're not my type."

Shamhat tapped their leg on the floor imperiously and pointed at her ripped pants.

"Yeah, yeah, I know," the aviatrix replied. "You seem to have a slightly less potent version of Tash's venom. But it's not going to make me horny enough to overlook that you're a bloody insect!"

The fae lights of Shamhat went white as they waited.

"Are you even intelligent enough to not make this creepy as hell?" Charlotte asked after a moment. "No kids, no animals. Those are the basic restrictions of the Art. I mean, we fuck the Dolls, but they're sex toys, not thinking beings, little more than walking dildos. Well, except for Tash. And you're obviously smart enough to be insulted by being compared to an animal, but without words, without conversation, how in Lilith's name can I be sure?

"Then again, what would count as proof?" the aviatrix grumbled. "Is there a crossword puzzle or riddle you can solve that indicates sufficient sentience for sex? I mean, your venom alone says you were designed for seduction, so unless the people who built you were some seriously sick bastards, you'd have at least human-level intelligence. Hell, for all I know I'm like an animal to you, and you're the one who views me as sub-sentient.

"Argh! I feel like I'm taking crazy pills," Charlotte exclaimed in loud frustration after a couple of minutes of the staring contest and debating herself. Shamhat stood still, occasionally peering over at the fae light it had pointed to. In that short span of time since falling it had dimmed to nearly nothing, lying on the ground like a fading campfire ember.

"Okay, okay, fine!" Charlotte relented. "We can try. But I think you're just wasting time and power. The more I think about it, the less attractive you get."

Shamhat's lights turned a deeper purple, and the ivory-shelled machine skittered closer. Charlotte repressed a shudder as the feather-light automaton clambered up her leg and body, moving around to her back. She wasn't sure there was any amount of seductive venom that Shamhat could secrete that would overcome her instinctive revulsion at the insectile form.

The automaton was careful this time, and the cautious hesitancy with which they settled on Charlotte's back as the six golden legs wrapped around to the front would have been endearing if the aviatrix hadn't been fighting the urge to knock Shamhat off and stomp on them.

Charlotte shut her eyes tight, trying to conjure images of Tash, of Lauren, of anyone she'd ever had sex with. Shamhat's hind and mid legs contracted around the bustier of her flight leathers like an external herringbone reinforcement, applying a gentle pressure. Shamhat's forelegs curled under Charlotte's moderate breasts, perking them up with careful support from below. The aviatrix clenched in instinctual anticipation of a sting as Shamhat's tail moved outside her field of view.

Charlotte yelped in surprise as the tail slid between her legs.

"Whoa, hold on, let's not get too crazy," she objected, swatting at the end of the scorpion tail as it rose between her thighs. Shamhat had narrowed their tail, using the mass to extend it up and out in front of Charlotte like a swaying alien phallus. "I hope you don't think you're going to stick your key-things in me. That's not going to happen, sugar."

The aviatrix turned her head to see what color lights Shamhat was responding with only to be startled by meeting the deep purple fae lights in a direct gaze.

The modified automaton had protruded their head from the narrow shell of the body, resting it softly on Charlotte's left shoulder and gazing steadily at her. Before the aviatrix could repeat her denial, the scorpion tail curled back around her mons and belly, snaking up to lock into place with the clutching legs that formed a golden bustier with a strap that ran between her legs.

Charlotte gave a low whistle of appreciation. Shamhat's embrace was accentuating all the right places, giving her an hourglass shape that nonetheless was as comfortable as going nude. Her breasts were perky and supported, and she could feel Shamhat making micro adjustments as she moved, giving Charlotte all the benefits of a corset with none of the drawbacks. The flattened tail that ran between her legs was warm and firm against her and looked more like a strap from some very kinky golden panties. The effect over her scarlet flight leathers was both lewd and comforting at the same time.

"Um…well, this is certainly an interesting fashion choice," she half-joked. "While this is quite lovely, and surprisingly functional, I confess I'm not quite sure how transforming into gilded lingerie is going to solve our problem."

Charlotte was trying her best to not succumb to the claustrophobia that had plagued her for all her life. Shamhat's legs had flattened where they gripped her, the gold alloy retaining the malleability of their constituent elements. Tiny needles pierced Charlotte's flight suit, injecting miniscule amounts of the rapturous venom. Shamhat's head retracted back, and the modified machine nuzzled along her spine, spreading warmth and peace where they touched.

Despite the alchemical help, it was difficult for Charlotte to settle her mind and turn it to more erotic thoughts. Even as she fought back the half-realized fears lurking at the edge of her mind, the aviatrix became irritated with herself. She had asked Shamhat to help, and despite spurning and insulting the machine, the little manticore was still doing their best to comply with her wishes.

"Okay, Char, get yourself together," she whispered to herself. "You need to help generate the energy. The key won't work if the lock won't turn."

But after a few moments of trying, Charlotte began to despair of getting in the mood. Unlike Tash, the venom that Shamhat used was relatively low in potency, at most helping add a rosy tint to fantasies. Although she counted herself lucky that Shamhat's sting didn't carry the same mind-controlling properties of Tash's, it would have come in handy in this instance. Even using her meditative breathing didn't work. Nothing was getting Charlotte in the mood; there were simply too many worries and fears crowding in.

"I'm sorry, Shamhat. This just isn't happening," Charlotte said, bitter defeat at the edge of her frustrated words. "We're going to be trapped down here forever because I suddenly lived up to the name of Captain Frost."

The purple glow from the hidden machine flared bright enough to light the area for a moment, lengthening Charlotte's shadow and taking her by surprise at its intensity. She felt Shamhat moving again, and an audible thrum filled the cavern.

Nestled firmly against her sex, Shamhat's tail began to vibrate.

Chapter 4

Charlotte's eyes went wide as the vibrations from the scorpion's tail resonated through her pussy.

Her anxiety tried to fight against the stimulation, a battle that Charlotte joined with meditative breathing and determination. Although she'd used vibratory devices before, including a feature on the latest Dolls, what Shamhat was doing felt altogether different. The aviatrix closed her eyes again and concentrated on the sensation and realized that Shamhat was subtly altering the frequency, tuning it to each involuntary shiver that ran through Charlotte's body.

"That's...very nice," she breathed, tension releasing as the vibrating tail coaxed not just her clit, but her entire sex. Her labia were also being luxuriously massaged through the flight leathers at a different rate, bringing a sense of comfort along with the intense stimulation from the center. She felt the first orgasm coming, a small prelude of what was promised by the all-encompassing vibrating tail.

Half-imagined fantasies and memories swirled in her mind, frozen in time like frames of a zoetrope. The pictures spun around and around, and she realized her point of view was pulling back. Like blades to a rotor the images solidified into a single whirling mass, held in place by ghostly hands above and below them.

Charlotte looked around with surprise. There was light everywhere, bright but not blinding, a world of hollow outlines. No color seeped into the world, but she could clearly see the confines of a phantom cavern, soft black outlines showing her immediate environment of the brick temple wall as well as the crashed *Lilith's Embrace*. The ghost world faded away after about ten feet, an infinite glowing white.

In the center of the vision an androgynous being, bereft of any defining features, spun the memories and fantasies above their open palm like a card sharp looking for aces from the hovering mass. The entity was as hollow and undefined as the world, but Charlotte could sense their surprise when they looked up and noticed the aviatrix watching them.

"Situation: unexpected."

The voice came from everywhere around Charlotte, but she knew it was the hollow person speaking.

"Um," Charlotte said. "Hi there? Are you...are you Shamhat?"

The entity nodded their head as features appeared on them. Eyes, nose, mouth, ears, all seemed to slowly fade into existence, although it was still impossible to tell a definitive sex or ethnicity.

"Greetings: Human-Who-Repairs-And-Modifies."

Despite the oddity of the situation, Charlotte couldn't

keep from barking out a laugh at the earnest way Shamhat named her.

"You can just call me Charlotte," she managed through her humor.

The phantom bobbed their head. "As you wish: Charlotte-Who-Repairs-And-Modifies."

Before Charlotte could correct them, she saw the mischievous gleam in Shamhat's eyes.

"I walked right into that one, didn't I?" Charlotte laughed.

"Confirmation: little bit," Shamhat replied with an impish grin.

Charlotte gestured around to the phantom world, made even more stark by the lifelike images frozen on the rotating zoetrope Shamhat bounced in their hands. The rich reality of the spinning images never touched the hollow hands, floating above as if a magnet repelled.

"What is this place?" Charlotte asked.

"Location: extrapolated from sensory input," Shamhat replied. A puzzled frown passed over their face. "Admission: perception capability surprising."

"Oh, yeah, I'm all kinds of special," Charlotte said in a dry tone. "I've received a bit of training in this kind of thing. I assume that we're in some form of shared mental construct where you're trying to find what gets me off so we can unlock this door."

"Training: beyond normal practitioner," Shamhat said in obvious admiration. "Caution protocols: engaged. Informational sharing: limited."

Distantly, as if an echo down a canyon, Charlotte felt

the vibrations continuing, the physical stimulation growing in her body. But here, in the ghost world, the sensations were muted, deadened.

"Why did you bring me here?" she asked. "If we're trying to generate tantric energy, pulling me out of the moment is not the way."

Shamhat shook their hollow head. "Corporeal disconnection: unintended. Counterproductive: sexual generation dampened. Total power loss: twelve minutes forty seconds."

Charlotte fought back the frustration that gnawed at her.

"So, we've only got a few minutes before you run out of juice?"

"Clarification," Shamhat said, sadness creeping over their expression. "Power loss: shared. Deactivation of Charlotte unit: imminent."

Charlotte took a few precious seconds and screamed out into the white void surrounding them.

"I'm going to die too if we don't get the suppression field turned off?" the aviatrix asked through gritted teeth. Shamhat nodded their head.

"Well, that's just fucking lovely. Dying with a scorpion corset in a dark cave was what I dreamed of as a little girl."

Shamhat looked insulted. "Negative: unit Shamhat is not of order Scorpiones. Original frame type: Enkidu worker unit. Current frame type: designation not yet assigned."

Charlotte pinched the bridge of her phantom nose and

tried to keep her temper. "Enkidu, scorpion, whatever. The point was me dying."

"Mortality: the state of all that lives. Confusion: Charlotte unit unaware of this?"

Charlotte opened her eyes, ready to scream at the ghostly machine in frustration. But the impish smile on Shamhat's lips was back.

"You're a real bitch, aren't you?" the aviatrix laughed.

Shamhat's glowing form grew thinner in the middle and thicker through the thighs and breasts, growing an impressive pair with nipples that popped into existence.

"Seduction mode: Shamhat can be whatever is required," the suddenly very feminine voice of the hollow woman said.

"I guess Tash had to learn it from somewhere," Charlotte replied, shaking her head in wonderment.

"Clarification required: Tash? Similarity to human temple naming convention: noted."

"A Doll," Charlotte started, then stopped herself and started again. "Or at least I thought she was. Is? Between her and Arslan who, yes, I know, is also part of the temple naming convention...you see, originally, I thought they were some advanced prototype the Matriarchy had been working on, but then—"

The features of Shamhat suddenly disappeared completely, leaving only a blank oval where the face had been.

"Emergency information blackout: initiated," droned a voice without any inflection or emotion.

"Wait, what?" Charlotte asked, confused. "What did I say?"

"Processing: alternative repair options."

The aviatrix could feel a minor orgasm at the edge of her senses, but despite the vibrations of Shamhat in real life without a soul's connection she knew it would generate barely any energy. Mentally reviewing what she'd said, Charlotte had a realization.

"You don't much care for the Matriarchy, do you?" she asked the blank oval. There was no response. "I'm not accustomed to being ignored. Shamhat—"

Charlotte reached out to shake the hollow woman's shoulders, but her hands passed through the outline of a woman without touching anything.

"That's concerning…" the aviatrix said. "Is it just you, though, or…"

Testing a theory, Charlotte tried to move within the limited confines of the void, meaning to go to the wall and touch it. But despite her feet moving, she remained firmly rooted at the center of a tiny universe.

"Judgment process: complete."

Although she tried to stay calm, Charlotte could not keep the irritation out of her voice. "Oh, really? How nice for you. If you would just listen for a minute, I could have told you that me and the Matriarchy aren't exactly on friendly terms right now."

Shamhat's female face reformed, although there was no trace of mirth or impishness, only a stern and serious look. She raised a hand to forestall any other words from Charlotte. "Protestations: irrelevant. Worthiness of claims or vows from Matriarchy units: laughable. Restriction level reevaluated: white. Behavioral protocols: adjusted."

Charlotte was starting to wish she could strangle the outline of a woman and reflected that perhaps it was a good thing she couldn't touch the hollow woman right now. "I'm guessing 'white' level isn't great?"

"Information availability: child."

"Wonderful," Charlotte snapped. "That's very helpful. Keeps me in the mood too, being compared to a kid. Superbly sexy talk you got there, sugar."

"Total system shutdown: eight minutes forty-three seconds. Former complaint duration: nine seconds. Recommendation: less complaining."

The aviatrix really wished she could punch a very specific thing. She took an imaginary calming breath, believing as hard as she could in it to try and make it real.

"Fine," she said with an edge to her voice. "We need each other, and you're soured on me. Got that. But you're making a mistake, Shamhat. I just stole away the Matriarchy's prize Doll and stumbled on a secret I'm pretty sure the Legion of Lilith would kill me over. So, if you could just show the tiniest bit of trust so we don't both die, well, that would be just *dandy*."

The hollow woman's expression didn't change. "Refutation: acknowledged. Evaluation protocols: initiated. Clarification: timeframe exceeds current operational future."

"Yeah, yeah," Charlotte grumbled. "It's going to take time to trust me. Got that, too. But for now, can you put me back in my body so we can both not die?"

Shamhat gave an uneasy shrug. "Hesitant confirmation: this unit will try. Clarification: process dangerous."

It was Charlotte's turn to shrug. "So is damn near everything else in life. But it's not like we got much choice in the matter, right?"

Shamhat nodded. "Confirmation: deactivation imminent."

The hollow woman held her hands out, palms up. Taking the hint, Charlotte reached out and covered Shamhat's hands with her own. The black outline of a woman shimmered in their shared mind's eye, the lines of her form blurring and taking on a reflection of Charlotte's body type. Sensing what was coming, the aviatrix steeled her nerves as the hollow mirrored shape floated forward into her.

A shiver rolled through her mind and body as Shamhat turned around, aligning her stolen form perfectly with Charlotte's. There was no sign of the hollow woman now, her insubstantial ghost substance perfectly aligned with the aviatrix. The world felt as if it were dropping out from under her, and Charlotte's heart leapt as the instinctual panic of falling kicked in.

Charlotte's eyes opened to the real world.

There was a scream coming from her throat, equal parts shock and ecstasy. The mechanical corset that Shamhat had fashioned out of the modified Enkidu she'd possessed was vibrating along Charlotte's spine, her sex, and under her breasts. There were waves of tantric energy matching the frequency warming the aviatrix through her scarlet flight leathers, comforting and arousing her simultaneously.

Charlotte reached down with her fingers, seeking to pleasure herself as well, but the scorpion tail was wrapped firmly around her nether regions. She moaned and bit her lip, mewling at being denied access to her own sex. But rather than douse her mood, the tantalizing denial as the vibrations continued heightened the experience. She could feel the smaller orgasms were just the precursor to something bigger, building at the back of her mind like an earthquake rumbling.

The panel was still open on the wall, waiting for the insertion of Shamhat's tail. Charlotte grabbed hold of the depressions in the panel, using it to steady herself as Shamhat relentlessly vibrated against her pussy.

Words failed her as the pressure built up, a flood held back by a fracturing dam. Several times she was close, right on the edge, and Shamhat backed off the vibrations, leaving the aviatrix hungry and growling in frustration.

When the Enkidu's tail began thrumming again Charlotte could feel the difference, a tiny adjustment of frequency and pressure. Somehow, she knew this was the one, that Shamhat was going to take the aviatrix all the way this time. Pleasure bordered on pain as her overstimulated clit responded to the vibrations like a starving woman offered food.

"Fuck, fuck, fuuuuuuck!" Charlotte screamed as she began to cum. The vibrating tail kept thrumming relentlessly, taking her to the edge of madness as her knees buckled and the hairs across her body stood out as if she'd taken a lightning bolt to her soul.

There was a click as the Enkidu tail disconnected from where the golden legs were supporting Charlotte's breasts. The multiple prongs on the end were glowing deep purple with the tantric energy from captain's orgasm.

Charlotte pulled her hands away just in time as the scorpion tail thrust forward. The shimmering prongs on the end slid easily into the lock. With a twist one way and then the other, there came an audible click from the panel.

The aviatrix stumbled back, the force of her orgasm still sending aftershocks through her body. Her knees were weak, and she was barely able to keep her feet. A hunger for more still warmed her loins, but she wasn't sure she could stand another orgasm so soon. When Shamhat pulled the scorpion tail free from the lock and reseated it as the front of the corset the vibrations disappeared. Charlotte found herself caught between relief and disappointment that the gold and alabaster Shamhat had become still again.

For a moment, nothing happened, and the recovering aviatrix began to fear that whatever mechanism the panel was connected to had been lost to age and disrepair. But then a rumble suddenly sent up a cloud of dust, quickly corralled again by the floor's electrostatic current.

The rectangular outline of a giant section of the wall at least thirty feet high and half again as wide appeared as the massive slab of stone pushed out a few inches. The thick section of wall split down the middle as the twin sections began opening outward.

Light spilled out from inside, overpowering the dim fae

lights and blinding Charlotte for a moment. Her eyes struggled to adjust to the sudden illumination; she could tell that the corridor beyond was of the same gigantic proportions as the hidden door, built to accommodate the monstrous Enkidu.

As her sight recovered from the sudden burst of light the aviatrix noted that the light came from the surface of the blue-glazed wall, the effect almost believable as a cloudless afternoon sky. The hallway beyond was relatively featureless beyond the carved decorations under the glaze, running only about a hundred feet before another set of doors barred the way. There was no sign of dust or dirt inside, and the carvings showed no evidence of the heavy weathering that had taken a toll on the cavern Charlotte stood in. She didn't need the perceptor monocle to feel the thrum of magic running through the corridor, feeding out to the cavern's suppression field.

A quick whispered incantation recalled the trio of remaining fey lights, bringing the marbles home to roost in a belt pouch. If she could turn off the suppression field then the others could be recovered at her leisure.

When Charlotte entered the hallway it felt as if she stepped from dry land into a bog. Every footstep forward was an effort, the suppression field increasing with every inch she pushed into the glowing corridor. This was the heart of the deadly entropy, the place that was siphoning off the magic of life from both her and the constructs behind.

There was something ugly and wrong in a heap at the end of the odd hallway, the only imperfection marring the breathtaking architecture. The hairs on the back of

Charlotte's neck stood on end as she approached the foreign object. As her eyes fully adjusted to the brightness of the corridor, Charlotte's breath caught in her throat. The aviatrix felt a knot of alarm form in her gut, stronger than even the suction of the suppression field.

Death stared at her from the eyes of a corpse, a warning to any who would dare trespass into the ancient ruins.

Chapter 5

The corpse was that of a woman, mummified by the arid environment, wearing a patched peasant dress. The dead woman's hands were wrapped around some sort of lever protruding from the wall, and from the way she had collapsed it was obvious pulling the handle had been her final act. The corpse had died with her back to the wall, her sight firmly fixed on the cavern with her hands locked on the lever above.

The corpse was remarkably preserved, and if it had started moving Charlotte wouldn't have been surprised. But the dead eyes and face showed no sign of motion. The woman's face had a peculiar look of triumph to it, a rictus of a grin that held no remorse or second thoughts.

Charlotte put on the preceptor monocle, careful to avoid touching the corpse directly. The dull throb of magic pulsed around the body; the suppression field was even stronger here. Tracing the lines of power with the monocle, the aviatrix was unsurprised to find that the energy was more virulent around the handle the dead woman had been so intent on pulling.

"What was so important that you'd sacrifice your life?" Charlotte asked the corpse. "The Enkidu? It wasn't even in the corridor with you. Or were you the last woman out? Did you pull that lever knowing that it would end your life?"

Analysis: correct.

Charlotte nearly leapt out of her skin at the ghostly reply. For a moment, she thought the dead woman had answered her. But after a heartbeat she recognized the cadence and tone of the disembodied voice. Her hands automatically went to the mechanical alabaster and gold corset that had formed around her midsection.

"Shamhat?" Charlotte asked hesitantly.

Supposition: correct.

"So, what, are you just going to be a voice in my head from now on? I didn't give you permission for that, sugar."

Explanation: soundwaves transmitted via physical contact.

"Head, body, whatever. I don't suppose you'd like to educate me on why you and yours turned against the Matriarchy? There's no way that they could build the ships and city parts in the cavern without your assistance. And, unless I miss my guess, the first aviatrixes were trained by your builders. So, why the change of heart?"

Silence greeted her.

"Wonderful. You're only chatty when it makes me jump out of my skin in fright? Classy move, sugar. This part of your observation? You want to see if I've got the brains to puzzle it out, and whether I feel sorry for the aviatrixes that died? Well, I don't know about the smarts bit, but I do know that needless death of any kind pisses me off. Did they even know why you turned on them? Did you bother explaining it?"

Crone Council: warned. Time until expiration: three minutes seven seconds.

"That's a hell of a way to change the subject," Charlotte groused. But she realized the mechanical intelligence had a point. There would be more time for questions after she shut off the suppression field.

Whatever was generating the field lay beyond the wall the corpse was slumped against. That the handle the dead woman was holding on to had activated it was obvious, but there was no assurance that it could turn the field off if flipped. The deadzone was strongest around the handle; activating it had undoubtedly killed the aviatrix who'd stayed behind to pull the switch. Touching it, even with her own magic primed, was likely as not to be lethal to Charlotte. But she didn't have much choice. Already the physical effects were beginning to pull at her, an exhaustion she could feel in her bones. Life itself was a form of magic, and as tenacious as it was even it would be drained off by the field if the leech wasn't pried loose.

Knowing that flipping the lever up would be pointless if the dead woman weighed it down again, Charlotte held her nose and toed the corpse's grip off the handle. Decades of desiccation had loosened the grip, and the hands slid off without much trouble. Charlotte held her breath, expecting the smell to overpower her. But the arid environment had mummified the corpse enough that the more disgusting aspects of disturbing the dead were missing. Charlotte whispered a small murmur of thanks to the Syrian Desert.

"That's enough dilly-dallying," Charlotte chastised herself. The deadly exhaustion was washing over her, her magic drained to its last ergs. "It's all or nothing now."

Concentrating on her work gloves, she murmured an incantation to help her center her mind. What power she had left she focused into her hands, using the crushed quartz within the glove lining to conduct the magic to their surface. Before she could second-guess her decision, Charlotte grabbed the lever.

Even with the protection of the gloves, it felt as if she was trying to wrestle an electric eel. The strangest sensation of suction from her hands threatened to drain her of all life as she pulled upward on the lever. Color seemed to drain from the world, and the aviatrix realized she was about to pass out. For a moment panic gripped her heart like an icy gauntlet as the handle refused to move. But then, as if a dam breaking, it suddenly shot upward with the force of her pull. Charlotte tumbled back onto her ass, barely missing the dead woman in her fall.

Suddenly, the world regained all its vibrancy, an almost painful intensity of color and sound. It was as if she'd been hit full in the face by a waterfall, the bracing and refreshing spray of energy reinvigorating her drained soul. The aviatrix became keenly aware of how much strength and magic had been siphoned off from her as she struggled to stand. A field long dry had finally been kissed by the spring rains, bringing life back to the soil that had lain fallow through the winter. She was still tired, but it was more due to the stress of the mystic forces on her body than from the leeching effects of the deactivated suppression field.

A door next to the handle hissed open, releasing the faint scent of old leather and vanilla into the hallway. Beyond the door lay another corridor with the glowing, blue-glazed walls that led to a T-section with hallways going to the right and left. The air noticeably changed, the humidity being that of a wonderful spring day with a temperature to match.

Suppression field: deactivated.

"Thank you, Captain Obvious," Charlotte smarted off to Shamhat. "That said, feels like I could use a nice, long nap. Still, I'd be lying if I said I wasn't curious about what wonders lie within the depths of this place."

Warning: reignition of Temple of Ishtar not recommended.

"Really? Because I think you're full of it. I think you *want* me to go against your so-called recommendation. You're trying to manipulate me, aren't you? Still think I'm some stooge of the Matriarchy, here to plunder your secrets?"

Silence responded, but Charlotte could have sworn she felt a guilty pang from the mechanical corset.

"Can't lie fast enough to keep up with me, eh?" the aviatrix asked. There was a sharp tone to her voice. Charlotte had been toyed with by people better at it, so her senses were keenly tuned to pick up manipulation. "Well, don't you worry, Shamhat. I'm going to find out what in Lilith's name is going on here. Not for you, or for the Crones. For me. I'm damn tired of others charting my course for me. Time to remind you all of what being a Liberty Ship captain really means."

Despite sleep tugging at her mind, Charlotte tromped

into the next illuminated hallway with a determined step. Briefly she considered returning to the cavern to try and reactivate Tash. But there was no telling how long the Doll would remain inert while recovering from the suppression field effects. With luck the automaton was already moving again, but curiosity about what lay ahead charted the aviatrix's path for her.

Rather than overly considering her choice Charlotte just decided to take the path to the left at the T-section. She remembered the sheer size of the secret tunnels she'd seen from the air and if she second-guessed every impulse she'd never get anywhere. But by always taking the left turn when she came to a fork, she knew that she wouldn't get lost and could always find her way back if she hit a dead end.

The dim sapphire glow from the glazed walls provided more than enough illumination to fight back any shadows, but the glow still felt dimmed to Charlotte. According to Shamhat the place wasn't even really activated yet, so the magic in the walls was at best a residual charge. A quick check with the preceptor monocle confirmed her suspicion that the glaze itself could hold and transmit far more power. The way the crystal matrices lined up within the translucent blue medium was exquisite in both its simplicity and effectiveness. The glaze alone could handle more than ten times the power being run through it now.

"Imagine all the wonders you could animate with that much power saturating the environment," Charlotte whispered, impressed by the sheer scale of what the walls implied. The Matriarchy had trouble producing more batteries and cabling for new ships; it wasn't the scarcity of materials, but rather the skills to manipulate them that limited the reach of the aviatrixes. A single wall from the hidden temple would provide the materials for an entire Liberty Ship.

"The Matriarchy did not abandon this place willingly, did they?" she guessed out loud, hoping to elicit a response from Shamhat. But the mechanical corset remained stubbornly silent. Charlotte gave a small mocking laugh.

"Have it your way, sugar. I'll figure this out. With or without your help."

After the first T-section she encountered several closed doors that refused to open to her presence or applied pressure. The carvings were different from the walls, and she could only assume that they were either private quarters or highly secured broom closets. The former became even more likely when she also found open spaces just beyond the closed doors that obviously served as some sort of common area. Low couches were spread along the wall, their purple silk yellowed and brittle with age. A single book sat on the end of one, its cover caked in the dust of time. Curiosity got the better of her, and Charlotte carefully blew the dust away. She was disappointed to find the beautiful calligraphy of Arabic lettering, and once more found reason to curse her inability to pick up additional languages. Lauren had been the multilingual one, easily switching tongues and cultures as they'd moved through the world together.

Charlotte continued exploring, trying to leave the thoughts of her ex-wife behind along with the common room. After another set of barred doors, she noticed the floor beyond lacked the same gentle blue glow she'd become accustomed to. As she stepped onto it, she disturbed the light dust and jumped back with fright.

The floor of the room was made of transparent glass, and an army of Enkidu lay at attention below her feet.

Overcoming her initial fright, the aviatrix kneeled and brushed away the light coating of dust to get a better look. This was the first time that Charlotte had seen one of the monsters not squashed under an airship, and the sight made even her stout heart skip a few beats. Although the space below seemed relatively huge, the gigantic Enkidu filled the room with their scorpion-like forms. They sat alertly like chimeric lions guarding their pride, tails curved over their bodies, silent sentries that looked as if they could leap from their resting places at the slightest provocation. Charlotte pulled a small collapsible spyglass from her tool belt, allowing a closer view of the monstrosities without breaking through the floor.

She'd been close in her estimation of their massive dimensions, but seeing the real thing was an entirely different experience. The Enkidu were each the size of a healthy horse, and despite their alien nature the aviatrix couldn't help but compare bits of them to a natural world that they did not belong to. The automatons each had four legs, but the legs themselves were segmented into the smooth alabaster plates, a line of gold at each hinting to the complicated gearwork within. Instead of paws, it looked as if each has an eight-fingered hand splayed at the end in four directions, the thick fingers paired up in each cardinal direction. Their mechanical bodies were thicker toward the front, where a dizzying array of armor plates formed a mane like a lion's. The head was vaguely feline in form, with a triangular nature that in the moon would mimic a lion's silhouette. But there were no actual eyes, or ears, the face four separate featureless pearlescent plates joined into the triangular formation. Thinking back to the wrecked monster in the cavern, Charlotte shuddered at the thought of the face splitting open to reveal a maw of teeth.

Although the builders of the temple were obviously engineering experts, Charlotte was still hesitant as she put her full weight on the glass floor. The readings from the aetherometer had shown the glass to be alchemically treated, much like the windows on the *Harlot's Promise*, and it was clearly meant to be trod upon. Yet it was still unsettling to take first one then two steps on a completely transparent floor. She crossed the wide room as quickly as she was able to, ears alert for any sound of cracking from the glass. Time had taken its fair toll on many things, and there was no way to tell exactly how old the tempered glass floor was. The best engineer could see their good work thwarted by centuries of disrepair.

Yet despite her fears, the floor held her weight without a single grumble or crack. The next room was another glass-floored room, although this one also held the lounging sofas at its perimeter. Below were more Enkidu, and Charlotte began to wonder at just how many of the monstrous machines the Temple had on its premises. Even if the cavern the secret complex was nestled in had been naturally occurring, the sheer amount of work to convert it into the secret base was staggering to imagine.

"Shamhat," the aviatrix said in summons as she crossed

a third room with more silent guardians below. "What exactly are the Enkidu? Can you at least tell me that? They're big enough to make me doubt any peaceful purpose, but I'm guessing they had a hand in the construction of the temple?"

There was a moment of silence before the disembodied intelligence responded.

Conjecture: correct. Enkidu: service frame capable of multiple tasks when piloted by worker soul.

"Wait, those things take souls to activate?" Charlotte asked, aghast at the thought. A myriad of questions and fears blossomed forth, and she was ready to quiz Shamhat on whose souls were to be used. But there was a tightening of the mechanical corset the intelligence inhabited, and Charlotte got the sense that Shamhat had accidentally revealed too much.

"So, you're just as fallible as us," the aviatrix said teasingly, trying to get Shamhat to communicate again. But the machine intelligence remained stubbornly silent.

Taking another turn led her to a blank wall. There was no sign of any door or secret mechanism she could find, so she returned to the main corridor and took another branch. Given the size of the complex she was beginning to regret not marking her path. Charlotte briefly considered marring the glaze with slashes, but quickly dismissed the notion. Even if she wasn't averse to scarring the beauty of the walls, the residual charge might be enough to give her a nasty shock too. And with guard dogs right under her feet, it encouraged visitors to be respectful on the integrity of the place.

The next chamber put a stop to any thought of vandalizing the temple.

There were a pair of Enkidu in the room, one to each side, their frames technically in a state of rest with the chest resting on the floor but their heads and legs tensed and upright as if ready to spring into action at a moment's notice. The path through the center of the room and the arrayed guardians was clear, but to the aviatrix it felt as if she was walking between two firing squads, rifles lined up at her head and ready to unleash death. With their crouched position, the Enkidu heads were the same height as her own. Charlotte couldn't help but to stare into each as she passed, the strange alabaster material refusing to give her any hint as to whether the automatons were active or not.

Every nerve in her body felt on high alert as Charlotte walked between the silent sentinels. Her eyes darted between each, watching for any movement, any hint that death was ready to spring.

Despite her fear screaming to run, the aviatrix tamped down her terror and traversed the room without incident. Stepping into the hallway beyond was like having stared down death and won, and the adrenaline surge made her legs shaky. The Enkidu had never moved, but their monstrous presence was more than enough to make a person recount every sin and wonder about whether their afterlife was sorted and ready. Charlotte thought of all the hypocritical bible thumpers she'd ever encountered and steeled her spine. If riffraff like that was ready, then so too was she.

Although she thought the worst was behind her,

Charlotte quickly reevaluated that assessment when she encountered yet another room full of the Enkidu. And then another. And another, on and on again.

This was more than a simple workforce.

This was an army.

Charlotte cast back in her memory for the image of the underground complex from the air, of the interlocking hallways and rooms. Although she wasn't blessed with the gift of total recall like other aviatrixes, enough of what she remembered synced up with what she had seen to send a chill of dread down her entire body. If even half of lower complex contained Enkidu there were hundreds of the monsters lurking under the Syrian desert.

"To what end, Shamhat?" Charlotte murmured, walking past another set of the monstrous automatons. "What are these really for? Who built them, and why?"

Silence was her only answer.

Another corridor, another room, and more guardians. The fear of the Enkidu was a steady, looming presence in the back of her mind. Her imagination kept wandering back to the pair that were free of their glass prison, waiting and able to rush through the complex at her. It had taken the Matriarchy sacrificing an airship and all on board to kill *one* of the things, and even then, the aviatrix had been able to reactivate a portion of it. What chance did she have alone against the monstrosities if they suddenly decided to take umbrage to her trespassing?

Charlotte nearly jumped out of her skin as something gripped her shoulder.

Chapter 6

"Captain Frost? Is there anything the matter?"

Charlotte had pulled the heavy wrench on her belt and leapt away, putting her back to the wall. She was breathing ragged and narrowed her eyes at the fool that had snuck up on her.

Arslan stood in front of her, in a well-tailored white suit with yellow accents to it, complete with a gentleman's silk white top hat. He had apparently taken control of the body while Tash slumbered, and the mass redistribution was clearly masculine in the sharp clothes.

"Did I startle you?" Arslan asked, the hint of a smirk at the edge of his mouth.

Although the male counterpart to Tash shared her body, he did not share the female soul's infatuation with Charlotte. It wasn't just that he was gay; there was an undercurrent of resentment that the aviatrix had caught from him the one time his personality had surfaced. Whether it was because she had been forced to trick his persona into remembering an old lover long dead and buried or whether he just didn't like the fact Tash had so easily fallen into a relationship Charlotte couldn't say. What motivations and aspirations could she attribute to a sentient automaton older than his memories, who shared a body with a female soul that was his opposite in many ways? Charlotte had wondered before if even Arslan knew what he wanted or intended.

"Yeah, you gave me a bit of a fright," Charlotte answered, hanging the wrench from her belt again and straightening up. "I didn't expect you to be the active one. Is Tash all right?"

The dapper machine flicked an unseen mote of dust off his spotless white coat, waving the question away. "Yes, yes, she is well. Merely recovering from the drain of the leeching field. I assume, of course, that you disabled it, and thus I can move, hmm? I thought as much."

Charlotte marveled at just how well the elegant suit fit the Doll. The coat accentuated his already-broad shoulders, and the pressed slacks seemed to cling to his buttocks as closely as any infatuated lover. The front of the pants cradled his impressive package well, and Charlotte nearly blushed at remembering the member hidden by the cloth. His yellow leather gloves were soft and pliable, matching the same shade as his hatband, small, knotted tie, and the shirt under the vest he wore. His own pearlescent skin shone bright, the silver runes highlighting his square jaw and the ruggedly handsome lines of his face. There was only one problem with the clothes.

"Where did you get the suit?" Charlotte asked the preening Doll. "I know for a fact we don't have anything like that in the dressing racks on the *Harlot's Promise*."

Arslan chuckled. "As if I cannot be relied upon to fashion my own apparel out of the scraps available. The ruffled dress Tash wore was a suitable basis, along with a piece here and there harvested from your ship stores."

Charlotte took a step toward him, her temper flaring. "Tash *liked* that dress. A lot. I can't imagine she gave you permission to cut it up, no matter how bereft of clothes you were."

"Calm yourself, Captain Frost," Arslan said with a smile. He turned and showed a series of clips on the seam of the trousers. "You see? These clothes are adjustable. When Tash next takes possession, she can enlarge the pants to fit her prodigious bottom. The jacket and short coat as well have modifications that will allow her to cinch them in at the shoulders and let them out for her breasts, although I fear her expansive bosom may prove too much for the short coat."

"That wasn't my objection," Charlotte growled, taking another step. The way he was sidestepping the criticism was getting on her nerves. "She liked the *dress*. Did she give you permission to tear it up?"

The smile Arslan gave was smug. "Of course not. How could she, in her current somnambulistic state? But you both left me little choice. She has held the body for the lion's share of the time since we've been online. Why should she have all the fun? A ship to travel the world, a lover right from the outset. It is positively enough to make the gentlest of souls jealous."

Charlotte was struggling to remain calm. "Is any of that her fault? Fate was kind to both of you, she just drew a better hand is all. Do you hold her responsible for her good luck? That's insane."

Arslan nodded, his grin growing crazed. "True. And yet. Here we stand. Did you know, that when you were awakening my memories of Kudurri I would be able to follow that thread back to the source? As I slumbered, the memories came unbidden. Far, far too many of them. You stirred the silt of the lakebed, and I followed the trail. And remembered all that I have lost. The dress was a tantrum, I will grant you. But what are we, if not our failings and the bitter taste of disappointment?"

"Be better," Charlotte said, gritting her teeth. "I need to as well. Look, I know it's been difficult for you—"

"You know *nothing*!" Arslan roared, stamping a foot in frustration. "You made me *remember*! Do you understand what curse that is? I remember someone I loved, someone who I begged to enact the Gilgamesh Protocol, someone who I lost millennia ago! Kudurri is nothing but bones and dust now, and you expect me to let you and Tash play without recompense, without knowing the price I paid, without paying it yourselves? I will *not* allow it. I refuse! The two of you will come to the same tragic end. I swear this! Do...do you hear me, Captain Frost? I...you..."

Arslan clutched his chest as if having a heart attack, his perfect face contorted in agony. One of his hands grabbed at his own throat, strangling him, while his other hand fought to pry the fingers loose. Arslan's face smoothed for a moment into Tash's features, angry, determined, before once more becoming the angular lines of Arslan. He collapsed to his knees, clawing at himself, ripping his short coat open and spewing its buttons across the floor.

"Fine," he growled, jutting his chin out as if ready to spit. "I...yield. For now. Stop damaging our clothes, you pernicious trollop. But you must promise me, soul sibling. Promise you will not offer it to the good Captain. I would rather see us both torn apart than grant her the boon my beloved was denied."

For a moment his features shifted again, the body mass changing, as the two shared personalities held a private conversation. How long it lasted for them was impossible for Charlotte to know, but it was only a few seconds for her.

Apparently reaching accord, the body mass settled back into a masculine form, and Arslan straightened his tie, pulling his open short coat straight. He ignored the missing buttons with the greatest aplomb.

"We...reached an agreement," he said offhandedly. Then he sneered. "Tash is still too exhausted to surface, but she sends her regards."

"I noticed," Charlotte replied dryly. Her own temper had subsided at watching Arslan fight with himself. "Care to clue me in on what the Gilgamesh Protocol is and why it's so important I don't receive it?"

A small, pained smile from Arslan was all the answer she got.

"Whatever," Charlotte sighed, pinching the bridge of her nose to prevent a stress headache. "Are you at least able to help with this infuriating Temple? I'm wandering through without a clue as to what I'm looking for, and it feels like the slightest step out of line will wake up the monsters."

Arslan bowed slightly, but still radiated hostility. "As you say, Captain. After all, we are all trapped here together. What, precisely, are you looking for?"

The aviatrix closed her eyes and tried harder to fend off the headache. "If I knew then I would have found it. We're, as you noted, trapped. How about a way to open the cavern to allow us to escape? Or perhaps the answer to what and who you and Tash are? Or even, and I know this is going to just blow the steam off your top, exactly what this place is and how it relates to the secrets the Matriarchy are apparently willing to die for?"

"Most of those require not access to the temple systems, but rather to me," Arslan said with the same humorless smile. "However, I am not particularly in a sharing mood. And, to be fair, most of my memories are still fragmented, the freshest being around two thousand years old."

"There!" Charlotte exclaimed, pointing at the automaton. "Start with what in Lilith's name you're talking about. This place seems ancient. You claim to be the same. How are you even functioning if it's been that long? I can accept that the Matriarchy pilfered magic techniques from the past. Scientists have long stood on the shoulders of those that came before to advance their understanding, and there's no reason practioners of the Art wouldn't do the same. But are you claiming your soul is that old, that the frame you are in has lasted that long?"

"This body is *mine*," Arslan stressed. "It's not some random Kurian-type frame. This was crafted specifically for me, to house *me*. Your precious Tash is the invader here, and her presence has caused all the problems. If I had my druthers she'd be offloaded to the nearest Enkidu and call it done."

Warning: transfer of type seven and above consciousness matrices to worker frame has a degradation value of eighty three percent. Procedure: not recommended.

"Good to know," Charlotte responded to Shamhat, before realizing that Arslan had no idea that the mechanical corset was speaking to her through the whispered contact with her body.

Arslan, mistaking her answer for him, visibly brightened up and grinned the sly way she'd come to associate with when he was trying to pull a fast one.

"If that is the path you wish to go, I would gladly assist the esteemed practitioner in the process," Arslan said through the smile.

"No, I don't think so. Tash wouldn't survive the transfer, would she?"

Clouds of anger swept across Arslan's face. "She is a thief! This is *not* her body, and I am not fond of sharing! She is not even a Kurian! Her presence has wiped several sectors of my memory; there is not enough space here for us both!"

"That," interrupted Charlotte, "that right there. What is that term you keep using? 'Kurian.'"

It was Arslan's turn to look like he was getting a headache. "How do I explain it to a primitive like you? What tiny words can I find to dumb it down enough to not make your limited meat brain explode?"

"Try me," she said. "I'm not as dumb as you seem to think."

Arslan threw his arms in the air as if beseeching the universe for assistance. "Your very concept of existence, of history, of the flow of time and base state of the world, is so askew that the only way you and yours have ever been able to comprehend it was by ascribing it to acts of the divine. The truth is so much more, and it would take years just to correct the misunderstanding imparted to you by your limited senses. Even the most learned of animal cannot understand the lessons of the butcher without bringing death."

Charlotte slapped the blue glazed wall next to her, bringing Arslan's rant to a stop and sending a glowing ripple through the wall. "Fine, then. Start small. What is this place?"

Arslan looked like he was truly struggling for a moment, whether to not laugh or cry it was hard to say. But the mechanical man took a believable approximation of a deep breath and nodded to himself as if coming to some sort of decision.

"This," he began, gesturing around them, "is a temple to the Mesopotamian goddess 'Ishtar.' Known to the Sumerians as Inanna, to the Greeks as Aphrodite, as Venus to the Romans. The culture does not matter, nor does the term. They all refer to a divine being whose territory is love and sex, and all the implications thereof. That is the human definition of her. To my people, the Kurians, this is something completely different, and we harvested the primitive emotions and rites associated with her worship to power this temple and others."

"To what end?" Charlotte asked. "This place is far too intricate and well-built to be unimportant, no matter how pompous you make yourself sound."

Arslan raised a single finger and smiled, a more genuine one than before. "There is truth to your supposition. This place was built by our Enkidu to serve as two things.

"The first is that we needed an outpost, a place to facilitate and trade with your kind. Although crude, your ancestors did have certain endearing qualities, and you are closer to the truth of reality than you know. After all, I did fall in love with one of your finer specimens, Kudurri. He was of such quality that I tried to bring him over to enrich us all. In many ways, I was more comfortable and in support of your kind than my fellows all those years ago. What you perceive as pettiness and bitterness is simply the result of having my body hijacked, of having my name and accomplishments stripped of me. Fragments of those memories are all I have, and it is difficult to parse through them, both emotionally and intellectually."

A blossom of pity for the irate automaton bloomed in Charlotte. Arslan had the tone of an outcast, of one who walked the paths others sneered at. She was all too familiar with the loneliness of that, and how much having a partner mattered there. And if her trick with the magical hand job before in their escape flight had caused fractured memories to surface, she could forgive the cattiness that a soul tormented by them would wallow in. How, she reflected, would she react if she remembered some of the good times with Lauren, none of the bad, and had to try and piece it together like a puzzle with pieces missing long after she was dead?

When she next spoke, her tone was much softer, much more understanding. "Arslan…is that really your name? Is there another that I should call you? Would that…would that help with the pain."

"Arslan will suffice for now." The Doll seemed to deflate in on himself, and the bitterness lacing his words directed inward now. "How can I begin to claim the entity I once was, when so much is missing? And no, I do not only refer to the parts of myself overwritten by your consort. So much was taken, so much is missing. I cannot in good faith claim the name once whispered by my beloved. For now, I remain Arslan."

Impulsively Charlotte crossed the distance between them and hugged Arslan close. He smelled of mustangs and the desert, a wild and exotic blend that was nothing like Tash. The cotton fabric of the suit jacket was stiff, and for a moment so too was the mechanical man. Slowly, with the hesitancy of an outcast seeking shelter in a storm yet fearing the lash of memory, Arslan's arms wrapped around the aviatrix in a grateful embrace. The Doll sobbed, a wordless soft sound of tears he could not shed, burying his face in Charlotte's shoulder.

They stood there for a moment, the flesh and blood woman embracing the automaton who felt too deeply for his own good, before Arslan broke their hug. His touch was firmer, not cruel, but clearly trying to regain some measure of self-control.

"My apologies, Captain Frost," he said, holding her at arm's length by the shoulders. His voice was measured and controlled. "The behavior I have demonstrated today is inexcusable. And yet I feel as if I need to explain, if only to redeem myself somewhat. The memories you brought back to me are precious; there is no cause for me to blame you for the missing ones that ache in their absence. Had you not taken the actions you did, had you not used me as you did, there would no one present for recriminations. The Matriarchy would have retaken us both, and there would be no 'me' to complain of the treatment. Yet in the time I slumbered within Tash, as you both cared for each other, it became as a living hell for me, an underworld of emotions and needs that my dreams swirled around."

"I...understand," Charlotte started, before shaking her head and stopping. "That is, I *think* I understand, at least in small part. You were awake only for a moment of time, and in that brief instance, we used you, used your emotions, to escape both our fates. And when you next awoke there was a bitterness burning in your belly, the sweaty anger after a nightmare rotted out what should have been a pleasant dream."

Arslan nodded, his mechanical face tugged with exhaustion. "An apt description, Captain. I cannot deny there is a part of me that has a visceral hatred for you, regardless of logic and explanations. That section is rancid, jealous of what you and Tash have, of what I remember having so long ago. I wish it was different, that I could reason my way past it. But that acid taste is pernicious, prevalent. I can only promise to try and keep it under rein and nibble away at it, a rat trying to bring down the wall mote by mote. I hope that is sufficient. For it is all I can offer right now."

Charlotte cracked a wry grin. "Does that mean you are or are not going to explain all that crap you were talking about earlier?"

Arslan gave a sharp genuine snort. "That is a fair assessment and ask. However, angry or not, bitter or not, many of the things I said still stand. Even making sense of some of the concepts I spouted is more like a reflex than conscious thought for me. We must bring your understanding to a place where you can do the same without sending you into an abyss of ennui from which there is no escape."

"So, you're saying you need to lie to me until I'm tough enough to eat the truth full-force?" Charlotte tried to make it sound light and airy, but there was an edge to her voice.

"Not quite how I would have put it. But to some extent…yes," Arslan said with an embarrassed shrug. "Were I to give in to the lesser emotions within me, I would try and break you with the facts, cold and hard like uncaring bullets. But I refuse to be that person, refuse to use the truth as a weapon. Whether by influence of Tash or my own predisposition, I cannot say for certain anymore. It is impossible that she and I exist together without one influencing the other. How much of me was destroyed when she came to inhabit us, I wonder."

"So, let me get this straight," Charlotte said, trying to understand. "You claim to be not hundreds, but thousands of years old? But most of your memories are either jumbled or lost. I suppose that makes sense, most people have trouble remember what happened last year, never mind last millennia. We'll circle back to that. So where, then, did Tash come from? I saw…something, earlier, when she was having troubles. And I struggled to understand how and why."

Arslan shook his head. "I do not know. My current set of memories begin about the time you brought us aboard your ship. There is only darkness and pain before that. But I cannot imagine the Matriarchy has the technical knowledge to create a persona whole cloth. Even my people were unable to do such a thing at our height."

"And your people, these 'Kurians'…who are you? *What* are you?"

"Not human. Older than you would believe. And your mind needs time to accept those two facts, completely and utterly, before we can go from there. Lack of sufficient processing time would lead to insanity. Unfortunately, there is precedent for that conclusion. Humans overestimate the capability of their minds to stretch, to accept new information at odds with what they perceive as hard reality. You have had entire stretches of your history where a single immutable fact was discovered and drove your species slightly off. Tash would not view it kindly if I inflicted that fate on you."

Charlotte tamped down on her irritation. Arslan was treating her like a moronic child, unable to cope with the truth. But at the same time, if he was trying to be helpful, perhaps there was some wisdom in not prying too deeply, too quickly.

"All right, so let's say I accept the fact I'm too delicate and fragile to take the whole truth at once," Charlotte said, trying to keep bitterness out of her voice. "Can you at least help with the mystery of this temple? Perhaps if I sidle up to the truth on the side it won't break my poor little mind."

"Yes," Arslan said, stretching the word as he furrowed his perfect brow. He adjusted his top hat forward, as if about to tackle a particularly vexing problem. "Do you know, captain, how I managed to alter your precious Doll's dress so quickly? Do you think that needle and thread are so central to any man who desires male company?"

"I...honestly didn't even think about it," Charlotte admitted. "With the juicy mysteries of this place beckoning, I missed that you would have to be a lightning touch with the needle to make such drastic changes in the half hour since the suppression field went down."

"Just so," Arslan said, taking off his yellow gloves with a flourish. He presented his hand, palm up. As Charlotte leaned in, the Doll's palm was suddenly alive with activity. Innumerable tiny golden needles, like splinters of wood, burst forth from the alabaster fingers and palm.

"Quite useful little things," Arslan explained, making them wave like iron filings as a magnet passed over them. "Incredibly delicate, controllable to the micrometer. I am, in some ways, my own sewing machine. But that is merely a hobby, of course, not their primary purpose."

Rather than waiting for Charlotte to ask the obvious, Arslan stepped back and slapped his hand on the blue-glazed wall behind him. He raised his head, eyelids half closed over the golden orbs of his eyes, as if concentrating.

A brighter blue glow rippled out across the glaze. As it passed the inscribed Enkidu it seemed as if the carvings danced and shifted underneath. Charlotte leaned close, fascinated by the change. Using the monocle and a different angle, she realized that the carvings themselves weren't changing. It was her perception of them; the glaze had altered to adjust the reflections of the Enkidu carvings underneath, like a prism splitting the sun, forming strange lettering that was impossible for her to read on the surface of the glaze. Following the brighter glow, she watched the entire wall turn into a shifting mass of foreign scribbles, indecipherable to her. It was like no other language she'd ever seen, not English, but not Arabic either. But from the pleased expression on his face, she surmised Arslan had no trouble reading the symbols formed by the glaze.

"Interesting," Arslan said, his head moving as he read the changing letters. "The suppression field was a jury-rig the Matriarchy did on their way out. What had started as a cooperative endeavor soured somehow."

Charlotte came up to stand by the Doll, reaching out a hand to the wonderous glaze. It was cool to the touch, showing no sign of acknowledging her presence for good or ill. She traced the featureless surface, fascinated by the reflected movement below.

"What could they have done to earn the ire of this place?" Charlotte breathed. She stroked the smooth surface, marveling at it. "Did they know they were losing favor with the temple? What could possibly be worth losing access to this?"

Arslan placed his other hand onto the glazed wall,

protruding the delicate golden needles from it as well. "There are large sections of data missing from the core."

"Is that your kind's calling card?" Charlotte asked dryly. "Is there any one of you that has a complete mind?"

Arslan sighed, and although his eyes were featureless orbs Charlotte could swear he was rolling them in irritation. "I assure you, Captain Frost, the lack of memories are an irritation to us, one and all. My time was before this complex, but from what I can tell this place and the army of Enkidu that built it were intended for a unique purpose beyond mere homesteading."

"Let me guess," the aviatrix chortled, her imagination running wild. "My tiny little meat brain can't possible fathom the wonderous reason?"

"Quite the opposite, actually," Arslan said, concern marring his features. "This temple is a facility we *should* have no use for. My people were more advanced than this, having outgrown such infantile concepts. Or at least I thought we had. According to the information I can access, this place was no simple outpost.

"It was a prison."

Chapter 7

Charlotte was at a loss for words. She had come to expect a level of pomposity and a certain amount of arrogance from the way Arslan spoke of his people. A prison indicated something altogether different.

"Blast, this system is being very uncooperative," Arslan said, his frown deepening. "If I did not know any better, I would say it is being deliberately recalcitrant and secretive. We are apparently in some sort of lockdown. Minimal power, many systems offline. The little trick with the suppression field drained the stores quite a bit it would seem."

Charlotte snapped her fingers. "Of course! That's what the field is meant for. I'd lay even money that it was how they kept the prisoners under control."

Arslan shook his head and corrected her. "Not prisoners. Singular. Only one entity was imprisoned here. The entire complex was built to keep her contained. A warden sprite was installed that watched over the subject, and an army of Enkidu if she ever found a way to escape."

"One person?" Charlotte said, frank disbelief on her

face. "You're joking, right? Those monsters, this whole place, for just one prisoner?"

"I never said she was a person," Arslan said, shaking his head. "In fact, I struggle to comprehend the name given to me. And I will not besmirch her by repeating it. My fellows must have been mistaken, or there are flaws in the data record. It could not be her."

"What about this warden you mentioned, the sprite thing? Can't you just ask it?"

Arslan gave a very human-sounding sigh of frustration. "If only it were so simple. The warden is offline as well, either broken or stolen."

Charlotte found her hand had wandered to the heavy wrench on her belt, a talisman of everyday familiarity in the ocean of strangeness she'd been plunged into. But as her finger caressed the smooth steel of the tool, she had an idea.

"Can't we just repair it?" she asked. "This warden, that is? Even if you don't want to get your hands dirty you can tell me what to do, where to poke and prod."

Arslan withdrew his hands from the glazed surface, letting the material settle down into its normal glow. He looked as if he was going to punch the wall in frustration but took a visible effort and calmed himself.

"If only it were that simple," he sighed. "I am not what you would call knowledgeable about this subject. I know enough to operate our technology, but little beyond that. My people live an idyllic life in many ways, allowed to follow our dreams and study what appeals to us. My own interests were in more esoteric fields. You are more likely to know what is broken and how to repair it than I. I never gave much thought to how useless my fields are when my subjects are naught but dust and memory."

Charlotte cocked her head quizzically. "Exactly what were you a specialist in, then?"

Arslan waved his hand airily. "Art. Culture. Fractal analysis of the concepts of beauty and love and the theoretical applications to what you call magic. It was part of what drew me to my Kudurri. We were so very different, even beyond our physical forms. In each other we found the completion of ourselves. But as lovely and exciting as my own fields of research were, they are woefully inadequate to the situation at hand. Even were I to possess my full faculties, I would be as useless as a painting to a starving man."

The aviatrix felt a need to console the Doll, but she didn't have the words for it. So, she tried a different tact.

"Look, I might not be one of your kind, Arslan, or even understand or believe half of what you say. But your mystic technology is obviously the forerunner of the Art we practice. If we can find the power source for the temple, there's every chance we can fire this place up. Maybe then we can figure out what they're guarding and why."

Arslan nodded. "If we can only bring the warden sprite back online, we can at least ask it whether the prisoner remains or not. Shamhat will have those answers for us. Captain Frost? Why have you gone pale?"

Charlotte's skin prickled with fear as realization washed over her. The mechanical corset which seemed so comfortable and snug beforehand now seemed like an implied threat. She realized, rather belatedly, that the intelligence contained within could murder her quite easily by simply squeezing her like a snake.

"Um," she said, her mind racing. She dared not move. "We don't have to go looking for the warden. I found her a while ago."

Arslan appeared puzzled. Charlotte slowly raised her hand and hooked a thumb at her alabaster corset.

"I'm *wearing* her."

Arslan's mood went from confused to concerned quickly as he realized what she was saying.

"I never thought to ask where you had gained your new apparel," he lamented. "I assume the intelligence is hidden within. Why has it not revealed itself?"

Charlotte waited with bated breath, her arms held out like she was wading in a swamp. After a moment more, there was a distinct click and Shamhat extended her head over the aviatrix's shoulder. The fae lights that served as her eyes were glowing a bright yellow, bordering on red.

Caution: unknown Kurian entity. Possible conspirator. Enact safety protocols.

"She doesn't know you," Charlotte said, translating the thrums she heard through her contact. "She's worried that you're here to free her prisoner."

Correction: prisoner escaped one hundred seventy-five thousand and six hours ago. Confirmed conspirators: Matriarchy.

"Captain?" Arslan asked. "You have gone even paler than before."

"Well, sugar, that would be the sickening terror," Charlotte said, her stomach doing somersaults. "I think we finally know why Shamhat doesn't trust the aviatrixes. They apparently helped whoever was trapped here break out."

"How did the warden escape its own data diamond?" Arslan asked, doubt clouding his features.

"She hasn't really said. When I met her, she was sand, dispersed through the hangar-cavern by the suppression field. I'm honestly surprised she hasn't upgraded to one of the full Enkidu we passed, or even found a frame like yours yet."

An ugly laugh erupted from Arslan before he could stop himself.

"The sprite is not one of my people. It is a mere construct, a sub-par intelligence given a task. A task which, it seems, it has failed in completely. Its mind would be insufficient to pilot a Kurian frame, perhaps not even a full Enkidu."

"*Her* mind," Charlotte corrected.

"What?"

"Hers, feminine," Charlotte said. There was a sneer on Arslan's face she didn't much care for.

"*It* has fed you improper information," Arslan said with a grimace of distaste. "The class D intelligences we use are little better than servants, passable in their duties, but with none of the dreams or soul that make up my people. I would liken them to animals, save that animals have independent purpose, primitive as it may be. Each of our servants is made to its task, no more, no less."

Charlotte gritted her teeth. "Every time, just when I'm starting to tolerate you, hell, maybe even like you, stupid shit like that comes out of your mouth. Stop that. Right now."

"I only meant—"

"I damn well know what you meant," Charlotte said, cutting him off. "The same thing everyone who thinks they're better than others means. The Matriarchy and your kind would get along splendidly. But have you even considered that maybe you're not so high above her? You said it yourself: this place, Shamhat, all of it, was after your time. You have no idea what she's capable of."

"Has it spoken up to contradict me?" Arslan asked imperiously.

"No," Charlotte sighed in irritation. "*She* has not. I've seen it before, though. You must get the abuse victim away from the threat and keep them away. Give them time to get their feet under them, to reinforce the defenses their abuser has spent a long time eroding. Even then, some can't quite pull it off. But that's not their fault."

"Are you inferring—"

"No!" Charlotte shouted, cutting him off again. "I'm fucking *saying*. I don't give a damn what you think makes you better than Shamhat, better than me, better than anyone. The moment you start spouting off about superiority you show just how inferior you are. The more you claim to be better, the worse you are. You've got your good points, and maybe you know a hell of a lot more about what we're going through. But if you keep talking down to me, to Shamhat, to anyone, I'll kick your lily-white ass up and down this temple."

Arslan's mouth was working like a fish gasping air. He was having trouble keeping up with the staccato insults.

"Well, if that is how you feel, captain, perhaps my assistance is no longer required," Arslan said stiffly.

"Not if you're going to be an asshole about it," Charlotte growled. "Give the body back to Tash and fuck off to the corner of your mind. Go sulk, or discover new memories, or whatever the hell you do when she's active."

It looked as if Arslan was going to argue for a moment. Instead, he reached down to his trousers and undid the clasps that kept the bottom form-fitting to his sculpted buttocks. He nodded his head at Charlotte as if conceding a duel.

The sculpted face began to flow and shift, smoothing out and growing slightly plumper. His shoulders drew in as if being sucked into the jacket while simultaneous breasts enlarged to the point of endangering the shirt's buttons, pushing the short coat to the side more. The posterior filled out, forming the hourglass shape of Tash as Arslan ceded his control over the form.

The tall silk hat drooped slightly over her eyes. Tash took it off and sighed in consternation.

"Really?" she asked, turning the hat over and examining it. "A top hat? Is that not a little bit ostentatious and egocentric?"

"I believe that's Arslan all-over," Charlotte said with a grin,

"Mistress!"

Upon seeing Charlotte, the Doll rushed to her side,

pressing her generous bosom up against Charlotte and batting her eyes coquettishly.

"Miss me?"

The aviatrix barked out a laugh. "More than you know. How much of the conversation did you catch between me and Arslan?"

"Bits and pieces," Tash shrugged. "I am frightfully ashamed of how he spoke to you."

"Doesn't mean he's wrong," Charlotte replied. Although one of the aviatrix's hands was busy with the joyful task of holding Tash close, the other was stroking her own alabaster corset. The machine had withdrawn her head into the backpiece at the Doll's approach. "Shamhat? You're still active, right?"

Confirmation. System power: minimal.

"Right. That," Charlotte sighed. She turned to Tash, who was wiggling in a provocative fashion. "Tash, please. As much as I adore the view, we have other priorities. Do you have any idea who the prisoner was here, or how to reactivate the temple?"

Tash frowned. "No, mistress. I have no recollection of this place, nor of any information that was not directly shared by my counterpart."

Charlotte nodded. "I thought as much. Arslan's time slumbering in your shared mind revealed more memories to him, healed him in that way. Have you accessed any new shreds of your past?"

"No, mistress," Tash said. "I am as bereft of the memories as before."

"Well, that goes toward confirming a theory of mine,"

Charlotte said. "I'm not comfortable sharing it yet, as it might delay your full restoration, but if I'm right, you have no memory of this place for one simple reason: you've never been here before."

"But, mistress, Arslan—"

"Hasn't been here either," Charlotte confirmed. "Yet he was able to access the magic here, to understand and postulate on it. Are you capable of the same?"

Tash stood away from the aviatrix, looking down at her hands as if they were strange new things. "Perhaps? There should be no impediment to accessing the same tools, now that I know they exist. I can, at the least, try."

The Doll placed her slender hands against the glaze of the wall in the same way that Arslan had.

Nothing happened.

"Well, it was a long shot," Tash said with an uneasy shrug.

"Tash."

"Yes, mistress?"

"I order you to access the temple systems."

"I don't think…oh…oh my…" Tash said, as ripples of light spread from her hands across the blue glaze. "I believe I am now connected to the temple."

Charlotte smiled. "Well, we know that your unconscious tries to make me happy. What does it feel like?"

Tash closed her eyes, breathing in as if she were human. "It tingles. The sensation is as if a thousand feathers were dancing across my palms, as if ball lightning bounced between my fingers. But there is more than that. I see displays in my head, informational blocks ready to be touched, to unfold their contents to me like a hundred books all at once."

"Can you figure out what Shamhat is hiding from us?"

Recommendation: discontinue line of inquiry.

"Yeah, no," Charlotte muttered as Shamhat extended her head again to rest on the captain's shoulder, eyes glowing a cautionary yellow.

"What was that, mistress?" Tash called over her shoulder, thoroughly entranced by the glazed wall and the mysteries it connected to.

"Nothing for you to worry about, sugar. Any luck on what was imprisoned here?"

"There seems to be some sort of security system, replete with levels of clearance, sub-directories of contingency plans, and a mass of tangled notes appended to each block of information. Whoever designed this was as paranoid as they were talented." Tash was clearly irritated at not being able to give satisfactory answers to Charlotte.

But the aviatrix was not surprised. "Prisons aren't exactly known for being open to the public. Safeguards come with the territory of guarding anything dangerous."

"Many of the informational blocks do appear to be stored in sections that have powered down," Tash said. "If we restore life to more parts of the temple, perhaps I could access them then."

"Then can you at least find us a way to their power generation room?" Charlotte asked.

Tash hesitated. "I think so. The location is under some of the heaviest restriction. Perhaps they feared that if the facility went offline their prisoner would escape?"

Charlotte nodded. "Makes sense to me. Give it your best shot."

For a few minutes more, Tash moved her hands across the wall, as if coaxing a reluctant lover to shed their clothes. Charlotte ignored the whispered warnings from Shamhat, who despite it was taking no action to keep them from their goal. The intelligence's apparent lack of effort at opposing them made Charlotte suspicious. Shamhat had demonstrated both the willingness and ability to prove a nuisance when she wanted to, and there were at least two Enkidu that she could call to for assistance free of the glass chambers. So why hadn't she? If the warden sprite's sole prisoner had escaped, then why wasn't she doing more to secure the facility and expel its intruders?

The questions became even more important as Tash removed her hands from the wall and informed Charlotte that she'd discovered the power chamber. With the Doll's guidance they moved quickly through the temple, avoiding side paths and rooms that Charlotte felt a lingering curiosity to explore. That could come later when they were sure they had the temple under control. The last thing she wanted to do was to come face to face with an active Enkidu that Shamhat urged to violence.

Tash led them to a set of double doors that took up the entire face of a wall. With a whispered passcode and her hand against the doors, Tash leaned in, pushing the weighty stone inward. It was at least a foot thick, and Charlotte whistled low in appreciation at the security measure. Without the code and a willing Doll, it would have taken naval cannon to blast their way through. Why, then, had it been so easy for Tash to retrieve the cipher and use it, when so many other aspects of the temple they were locked out of?

The power chamber beyond rivaled the airship cavern in size. Banks of crystal glittered around the perimeter of the room, rubies, sapphires, and emeralds held in a liquid black suspension. At a guess Charlotte surmised that they served the same function as the batteries aboard the *Harlot's Promise.* But rather than the vibrant colors she expected, the crystal banks were dark and lifeless.

Connected to the battery banks by thick cabling were three cylinders that stretched floor to ceiling, as if pillars of the room. They were massive, ten feet in circumference, and made of the same gold alloy that both Tash and the Enkidu used for their internal mechanisms. Inscribed on them were an intricate pattern of diamonds, twisting and twirling in a dizzying array of patterns. The middle column was ruptured and blackened, some disaster having befallen it in the past, its diamonds burst open like overripe fruit. The lefthand column was missing most of its diamonds, the patterns showing clearly where it should have the gems and was missing them. The only intact column, the righthand one, was as dark as the battery banks. Although she had no clue how they functioned, it was obvious that they served as the temple's power source. It was also obvious they were completely and utterly dead.

Charlotte gave a startled yelp as her mechanical corset suddenly started moving. The tail snapped free of where it had fastened in the front, the legs unfolding from where they supported her breasts. The aviatrix tensed, but

Shamhat simply leapt off her back, scuttling with her tiny, modified form across the floor.

"You know, I need to name your frame," Charlotte mused as she watched the mechanoid begin examining the cables and crystal banks. "Not as big as an Enkidu, but you seem to like the same scorpion-type form. Which do you prefer, Enki or Kidu?"

Shamhat looked back with her fae lights flashing white and turquoise.

"So, you don't care?" Charlotte asked. "Fair enough. Any preference from you, Tash?"

"Hmm?" Tash replied off-handedly. She was tracing her alabaster fingers over the dead crystal banks, causing them to glitter in the glow from the walls. Charlotte could understand that this, the heart of the complex, would fascinate the Doll. Her birthplace might have been in the glass pens below, churned out from the same hidden forges that crafted the Enkidu. The aviatrix reasoned that there wouldn't be that many hidden complexes like the Temple of Ishtar.

"Then again, for all I know, the entire desert is just window dressing for whoever these Kurians are," Charlotte said to herself, shaking her head in bemusement at the thought of a desert honeycombed with hidden passages and temples.

Shamhat had clambered up the blasted-out column, peering inside like a doctor at a patient. She extended her forelegs deep inside the interior and went motionless.

"Nah, you're too cute for either name," Charlotte said. She reflected that only an engineer at heart could label the little scorpion-like thing as adorable. "I can shorten it more. Ki? Needs a little more spice. Kiki frame? I rather like that."

There was no response from Shamhat, so Charlotte took that as she could name the little modified form whatever she liked. Curious as to what had transfixed the little machine so completely, Charlotte walked up and examined the column with her perceptor. The crystalline structure was indeed based on the structure of diamonds, although the cleavage and visual distribution was far too standardized to be natural. She gave a low whistle of appreciation.

"Synthetic diamonds," Charlotte breathed. "Nice trick. I'm guessing the other precious gems in the chamber are also artificial. It makes sense, you've got a kingdom's worth of jewels in this chamber alone. But why are you so interested in this burnt-out power column, I…"

The aviatrix finally noticed the line of marching sand specks between the kiki frame and the crystal. With a snap of her fingers, she put it together: the diamonds were the data crystals Arslan had mentioned. Which meant that the broken diamond-studded column was more than just a curiosity for Shamhat.

It was where she came from.

"A power source and the home of an intelligence?" Charlotte wondered out loud. "Does that mean you *are* the generator, or just its shepherd? Regardless, that would mean that every column houses at least one intelligence."

This was the crime the Matriarchy had committed, and why Shamhat distrusted anyone associated with them. The column missing its diamonds, the golden sculpture marred by the tools used to pry them out. That was the missing prisoner that Shamhat and Arslan were worried about. An artificial intelligence that was dangerous enough to warrant an entire facility constructed to hold it, two separate machines keeping watch over it, and an army of Enkidu in case she escaped. How had the Crone Council kept such a powerful tool hidden, the kind of artificial intelligence that warranted such extreme precautions from the Kurians?

Then it suddenly occurred to Charlotte: perhaps they hadn't kept it hidden. Perhaps it had been working side by side with the Matriarchy for decades. Charlotte's blood ran cold at the realization. She knew who had been imprisoned here, an intellect whispering corruption into the Matriarchy from the very beginning. It had taken up residence in the flying city that housed all the aviatrixes, an indispensable asset.

Godmother, the artificial intelligence that had watched over Charlotte since she was a little girl, was the missing Temple prisoner.

Chapter 8

The full implications washed over Charlotte, paralyzing her in her tracks.

Godmother had served as a surrogate matronly figure to the aviatrix for years, for decades. Charlotte had lost her mother, one of the first Liberty Ship captains, when she was only eight years old, soon after Godmother and the Matriarchy had taken to the skies. Although the intelligence was largely cold and business-like with most of the aviatrixes, she had taken a keen interest in the orphaned girl. Charlotte had grown up finding the hidden shadows of the city, places where no human had ever set foot, escaping the exasperated searches of her foster families again and again under Godmother's tutelage. In the dark alleys where she was safe, atop the lonely glittering spires that dotted the Amethyst City, Charlotte had received the secrets to the Art and been taught other tantalizing fragments of fiction and fact by the artificial intelligence. She had come to think of Godmother more as family than even the sisterhood of the aviatrixes.

But Godmother had lied to her.

Never in their lessons had Godmother ever confided in her about the Temple of Ishtar. She had been flawless in her lies to Charlotte as the child grew, perpetuating the same fabrication the Crones had told, that the artificial intelligence had been an unexpected byproduct of launching a city comprised of equal parts machine and magic. There had been no hint, no whisper, that Godmother was an escaped prisoner of the forerunners of the Tantric Arts. The secret seemed too big to keep, but somehow it had been, and the source of both the Matriarchy's power and its flying city had remained hidden.

"Two can keep a secret if one of them is dead," Charlotte muttered to herself. She thought of the deceased aviatrix in the corridor, the one that had rigged the suppression field to blanket the Temple instead of the prisoner column in the power chamber. Was that the fate of all that had known the truth? Had the Crones wiped out any that would betray them, either through subterfuge or assassination? It was too big, too dangerous, to take in all at once.

"Mistress, why do you think this one is dark?" Tash asked, the question cutting through the enormity of Charlotte's revelation. The aviatrix looked up, and her heart skipped a beat.

Tash had her hand on the column that still possessed its data diamonds.

"Tash, get away from there!" Charlotte screamed, her mind awakening to the danger. If the diamonds were meant to hold rogue machine intelligences, and there was only one prison column left, then there was every chance that the diamonds could activate and trap Tash inside of them.

"I do not understand—" Tash tried to say as Charlotte lunged forward, tackling her, and breaking the Doll's contact with the crystals. "Mistress! Captain! Let me up!"

Charlotte had pushed Tash to the ground, using her weight to keep the Doll pinned as she cast furtive glances over to the column.

"Don't be so stupid!" Charlotte chided Tash. "You don't have any idea what that column will do to you!"

Irritation warred with concern on the Doll's face. "And you do?"

"More than you," Charlotte confirmed, and immediately regretted as soon as she said it. There was a storm cloud darkening Tash's face.

"You have discovered the secrets of this place, then?" the prone automaton asked. There was a coldness in her tone. "If only I had access to someone with more knowledge than you."

"I, uh," Charlotte stuttered. "I mean, there's no telling how much Arslan shares with you."

"Oh, I am incapable of listening in on my other half even though we share a body?" Tash asked too-sweetly. "A pretty little fool who takes looking-after, as a child does?"

Charlotte hastened to get off Tash, offering a hand up to the Doll. She batted it away in annoyance.

"Look, I just don't think—"

"No," Tash interrupted. "You do not. Mark me, Captain Charlotte Frost. No matter the nomenclature I refer to you as, I am not the lesser of the two of us. Perhaps

I have led you to the thought that I was a delicate thing, to be taken care of, to be shielded from the outside world. Would you have me dissuade you of that notion?"

Tash rose, her movements as elegant as ever. There was a stiffness in her posture at being treated like a child. Charlotte saw it, but there was precious little she could do to change it now. She had unintentionally begun to regard the Doll as an inferior, too delicate to face the world that they lived in. That perceived innocence, that vulnerability, wasn't something Charlotte experienced in her day-to-day life. Groundlings treated her either as a frightening bedtime story to keep clear of or as a welcome devil, full of temptation and forbidden knowledge. Charlotte's ex-wife Lauren had exulted in the distinction and brought part of her superiority feelings to the relationship, often making Charlotte feel lesser, as if not knowing ancient Sumerian somehow made her less worthy of respect. Without meaning to, the aviatrix had brought a ghost of the same treatment to her burgeoning relationship with Tash.

Charlotte felt the sour eel lashing in her stomach, knowing she was the one in the wrong, but unable to admit it in the moment. She wanted to tell Tash how much she valued her, how much the vulnerability of heart the automaton had shown meant to her. How the trust the Doll showed her from moment to moment lightened her day and made her soul sing.

But the part of Charlotte that still fumed over her last relationship wouldn't let her back down.

"Look, there's no need to be a bitch about this," Charlotte said, and immediately regretted it as soon as she did. But it was out there, the ugly snake that had struck, and the shame burning on her face was easily interpreted instead as anger. Better to be mad than to take being talked down to, said the evil voice in the back of Charlotte's mind. Better to push someone away than admit the mistake and be vulnerable.

The clouds that had been gathering on Tash's face coalesced into a storm of pain. She shook her head, eyes squeezed shut as if holding back mechanical tears, and turned away from the aviatrix, stalking off beyond the massive columns to the other side of the power chamber.

Charlotte didn't have to hear the soft sobs to know they were there. She'd done the same thing to the Doll that Lauren had done to her, twisting the knife in the right moment for the most damage. Tash had stood up for herself, and Charlotte had emotionally kicked her in response. She'd snapped at the Doll without meaning to, more a gruff echo of her own insecurities than anything else. Lauren had been in the habit of using any misstep to bolster her own feelings at the cost of Charlotte's. But Tash was different. Despite being made of golden gears and ivory plates, the automaton's emotions were much purer than those of Charlotte's ex-wife. For a woman who'd been hurt by the person who was supposed to protect her, it was difficult for the aviatrix to adjust to having someone who didn't seek to one-up her at every opportunity. Tash had not sought to control Charlotte, only to tempt, to seduce…to comfort. That inherent vulnerability, that trust that Tash showed every time she spoke to her mistress, was peculiarly endearing and lovely. Charlotte found herself wanting to protect the Doll, to keep that spark of innocence and hope alive that she saw in the gilded gaze of her companion. Her surprising and unflinching loyalty to the captain was a welcome balm after the bitter betrayals Charlotte had experienced.

"I'm sorry," Charlotte said, hurrying past the columns to the silent Doll. She reached out to touch Tash's shoulder but held back at the last moment. "I've been on my own for a long time, but then you…no. No. Damn it. Any apology that has the word 'but' in it isn't worth the ass saying it."

Tash turned, keeping her distance from the captain's outstretched hand, but not retreating. Anguish still marred the perfect features, but there was a ray of sunlight at the edge of the clouds. Charlotte could see it, the urge to forgive her for all words and actions, that pure belief in the woman she called "mistress." The Doll was struggling, her own beneficent nature at odds with needing to defend herself against the person who had access to her heart.

It was a struggle Charlotte knew all too well.

"Please, Tash. I *am* sorry. Lauren smashed a lot of things in my heart on her way out. But you shouldn't be cut by the pieces left on the floor."

Tash reached out, her long and elegant fingers brushing Charlotte's hand. "She hurt you that much?"

"More than I realized," Charlotte whispered, her throat suddenly tight. "But I shouldn't make you pay the price."

Tash slowly drew her in close, a small bittersweet smile of understanding on her face. "Yet that is the fate of those who come after, those who truly care. Those who truly… love."

Charlotte tried to reply, but her face was flushed, and the words wouldn't come. Against her will she felt the tears roll down her cheeks.

"Oh, my sweet mistress," Tash whispered, pulling Charlotte in. The aviatrix buried her face in the ample bosom of the taller Doll as the tears came hot and fast in a way that they had not in months.

"No, no, this isn't right," Charlotte said weakly, trying to push the automaton away, her voice hitching. "I'm the one who screwed up, so why are you the one comforting me?"

Tash didn't allow her to break the embrace, instead cooing words and running a hand down the captain's back. Charlotte felt the Doll's instinctive control of magic warm her spine and muscles as Tash manipulated the chakra to soothe the aviatrix. Rather than fight the comfort so freely given, the aviatrix clutched her companion, burying her face back in the other's bosom. Warm and inviting, the magic that animated Tash made her metal skin as luxurious as silk, even through the white overshirt that Arslan had favored. Tash's delicate fingers stroked Charlotte's hair, playing with the raven-hued curls while leaning her head against the top of the captain's.

"I understand, mistress," Tash breathed. "As much as the world is new to me, so too has it changed for you in the same span of time. Both of us must endeavor to allow the other more lenience for mistakes and misunderstandings."

Charlotte looked up, her dark eyes glittering mischievously as she hiccupped a small laugh through the tears. "So, is that a 'yes' or a 'no' on me installing a scorpion tail on your butt?"

Tash playfully swatted the captain's shoulder. "Has my allure faded so quickly that you now wish for something more exotic?"

A part of her mind told Charlotte she was a fool for thinking of the Doll as a real person. But that internal derision was growing smaller and smaller, smothered by the burgeoning feelings toward Tash that the aviatrix was leery of admitting to.

Tash gently but firmly pushed Charlotte back. The captain's eyes were wet and swollen from crying, so the automaton reached into the pocket of the short coat and pulled out the buttercup-yellow handkerchief with a gentle smile. "Here, mistress. You are making me very wet, and not in a fun way."

Charlotte coughed a giggle as she took the proffered square of cloth, wiping her eyes and nose with it. Tash took it back and with a small flick of magic and an incantation snapped it clean and dry, folding it back into the pocket.

"So," Charlotte said, her sniffles finally abating as she gestured to the motionless Shamhat. "What do you think has her so entranced?"

"At a guess, based on information she has shared, I would say she is checking on her old host-form, making sure none of her was left behind."

Charlotte nodded. "Not bad; you *have* been listening. I'd guessed the same myself. Do you think she'd mind if we prodded the third column?"

Tash shrugged. "If she does, then she is free to tell us such."

They approached the intact power column again. To assuage Charlotte's worries Tash took off the jacket she was wearing and wrapped it around her hands so that there was a barrier between her hands and the column.

"Do you think there's another intelligence locked in there?" Charlotte wondered as they poked and prodded the gems.

"If we accept all that Shamhat has told us as fact, then it seems inevitable," Tash shrugged, wiggling one of the diamonds to see how securely it was fastened in the golden sculpture. There was no give to it at all.

"Do you think she's lying?"

"Innocent I may be, mistress, but I am not a fool," Tash responded, brow furrowing at the inset diamonds. "Shall we take the entity at face value when so much of this is shrouded in mystery? Even if we possess the predisposition to grant such, there is wisdom in considering the shadowed path ahead. These are perilous secrets we have stumbled upon. Arslan has not shared with me precisely what we are, assuming even he knows. I can feel his smoldering anger at my presence. If, as he claims, I am an invader in his body and mind, then I can grant he has cause for such irritation. That said, even if I depart, I suspect his missing memories would not be restored. Once you press something into the wet footprint the original will never again be the same; I suspect the same applies to our shared mind space. Once overwritten, the ink below loses its meaning."

Charlotte laughed ruefully. "And yet, here we are, poking and prodding and making more of a mark as we go."

Tash shrugged, offering the jacket so that Charlotte could protect herself as she explored the darkened power column. "What choice do we have, mistress, except to continue walking the path ahead? Answers are not behind us, and the failure to move forward could prove lethal. The future is dangerous, but so long as we have each other, I am willing to face it head-on."

Charlotte smiled and waved the proffered jacket away. Whispering the words of power, the aviatrix summoned the last of her fae lights from her satchel. The trio of orbs, two blue and one orange, floated free and bright from their resting place. With the suppression field turned off there was no danger of their deaths now, and they easily responded to Charlotte's directions. They each floated to a diamond and touched it as the aviatrix braced herself for feedback. But there was none, only a sense of waiting, of watching from within.

"Stand back, Tash," Charlotte said. "I'm going to try something."

Although her own magic was still drained, enough had regenerated from her emotional interactions with Tash that the aviatrix had a small reserve. She concentrated, seeing in her mind's eye a small flame. Using her ethereal connection to the fairy orbs she sent a minute pulse of mystic energy through each. The orbs flared, their glows increasing tenfold from the magic running through them. The data diamonds reflected the shine, magnified, and refracted within their depths.

At first, nothing happened. Charlotte continued to concentrate, pouring more and more energy in. Her reserves began to flag, but then she felt a warm hand take hers. She looked over to see Tash smiling at her. Trust was writ large across the other's face, and through the automaton's hand Charlotte felt the Doll sending her own magic into the aviatrix. Charlotte turned back to the power column and extended her free hand, sending the combined power into the fae lights.

There was a flash of light like heat lightning, and with a crack the blackened fae lights shattered, their pieces falling smoking from the diamonds.

The sudden cessation of the link took Charlotte by surprise, and briefly she felt guilty about breaking the fae lights. But the glow now steadily coming from the three diamonds they'd touched pushed other thoughts out of her head.

Slowly, haltingly, the diamonds closest to the trio began flickering to life, as if the embers of a dying fire had been blown upon. Within moments they were glowing a soft white light, and the diamonds closest to them began to flicker.

Over the course of the next few minutes the glow spread through the diamonds of the entire column like a forest fire taking its course. As each diamond ignited, the pressure of mounting magical energy increased like the heavy feel of a storm front before a summer rain.

"Tash, this is amazing," Charlotte breathed, checking the aetherometer on her belt. "This thing is doubling its output every few seconds. It's already putting out enough energy to power most of Godmother for a few days."

The Doll cocked her head quizzically. "But why awaken it, mistress? To refill the battery banks of the *Harlot's Promise* and open the cavern again?"

Charlotte shrugged. "Partly. Partly to see if it could be done. You said it yourself: the only way is forward. There's no use pussyfooting around and letting the past catch up with us. We must be bold. Certainty is the purview of those who chase us. If we're going to stay ahead of the hunt, then we're going to have to take chances."

Tash gestured at the still form of Shamhat. "What do you think she will make of this?"

"I don't know," Charlotte admitted. "She warned me off starting this place up again before. But she doesn't trust us or our intentions, and I got the distinct impression that despite her protestations she wanted me to disobey."

Suddenly, a red glow rippled out across the blue glaze of the walls around them, leaving purple shimmers in its wake. A loud, insistent chime started sounding from within the room.

"Tash?" Charlotte said, alarmed. "What's going on? Did I do something wrong?"

The Doll looked as surprised as her mistress. She opened her palm, extending the golden needles from within, and crossed to the closest wall. Tash pressed her and against it, interfacing with the Temple of Ishtar.

"Mistress!" she said, fright in her voice. "We are not alone! There are intruders in the ruins above!"

"Damn it," Charlotte said, shaking her head. "Who the hell would be out here in the backwards ass of the desert?"

Tash pulled her hand away from the temple wall. "I do not know. But the Temple has sensed hostile intent and avarice. If we do not soothe its alarm, the automatic systems will activate the Enkidu stored below."

Charlotte's blood ran cold at the thought of the monstrous automatons swarming out from their glass prisons. There was no telling what they would do. But given the alarms that grew louder, it was unlikely to be anything peaceful.

"Is there a way to the surface in the labyrinth of the Temple that isn't blocked by rubble?"

Tash nodded. "I sensed a way that seemed to be largely free of debris. It is by this path the invaders are threatening the Temple."

Charlotte laughed, a scared edge to it. "Then what are we waiting for? Sounds like we don't have long to try and neutralize the threat. Shall we?"

She held her hand out to Tash, who took it with a firm grip.

"Together, then?" the Doll asked.

Charlotte smiled at her, letting loose all the feelings she'd been trying to hold inside.

"Always," she promised.

Together, the mechanical woman and the human one strode forward into the mysteries of the future.

About the Author

Award-winning author Timothy Black was born in the Deep South where he hit the road at an early age and quickly learned it could hit back. Driven by an insatiable curiosity, he studied Geology, Astronomy, and the Occult, ending up with a degree in Philosophy that twists through his writing. After traveling the world to find his great loves he settled down in the Pacific Northwest, determined to craft stories that defy confinement to any single genre. A serial killer of coffee and whiskey sours, he stays one step ahead of retribution with a rebellious cackle and knowing wink.

Facebook: facebook.com/timothyblack.author/
Twitter: @Tim_RFP

The Tales of the Tantric Aviatrix
The Clockwork Courtesan
The Ishtar Ignition

Gearteeth
Published by Dreamsphere Books
Gearteeth
Judgment of Blood (fall 2023)

Also by Timothy Black
Published by Dreamsphere Books

Gearteeth
Timothy Black

On the brink of humanity's extinction, Nikola Tesla and a mysterious order of scientists known as the Tellurians revealed a bold plan to save a world ravaged by a disease that turned sane men into ravenous werewolves: the uninfected would abandon the Earth's surface by rising up in floating salvation cities, iron and steel metropolises that carried tens of thousands of refugees above the savage apocalypse.

Twenty years later, only one salvation city remains aloft, while the beasts still rule the world below. Time has taken its toll on the miraculous machinery of the city, and soon the last of the survivors will plummet to their doom. But when Elijah Kelly, a brakeman aboard the largest of the city's Thunder Trains, is infected by the werewolf virus, he discovers a secret world of lies and horrific experiments that hide the disturbing truth about the Tellurians.

When the beast in his blood surges forth, Elijah must choose between the lives of those he loves, and the city that is humanity's last hope of survival.

Available in ebook and paperback!

www.ingramcontent.com/pod-product-compliance
Lightning Source LLC
Chambersburg PA
CBHW022030170626
46808CB00003B/1135